ALL ROADS

ALL ROADS

stories

COLLEEN O'BRIEN

TriQuarterly Books / Northwestern University Press
Evanston, Illinois

Northwestern University Press
www.nupress.northwestern.edu

Copyright © 2022 by Colleen O'Brien. Published 2022 by TriQuarterly
Books/Northwestern University Press. All rights reserved.

The stories in this collection previously appeared in the following:
"Charlie" in the *Gettysburg Review*; "Valentine's Day" in *North American
Review*; "#" in *West Branch*; "Savant" (as "Sasha") in the *Laurel Review*;
"All Roads" in the *Texas Review*; "Nine" in the *Antioch Review*; "The
Fathers" in *Fugue*; "The Deal" in *Painted Bride Quarterly*; "Nell" in *Willow
Springs*; "Diretora" in *Passages North* (online); "The Cheesecake Factory" in
Beloit Fiction Journal; "Shopping" in *Litro Magazine*; "Here For" in *Wigleaf*;
and "Amends" in *Sou'wester*.

Printed in the United States of America

10 9 8 7 6 5 4 3 2 1

Library of Congress Cataloging-in-Publication Data

Names: O'Brien, Colleen, 1979– author.
Title: All roads : stories / Colleen O'Brien.
Description: Evanston, illinois : Northwestern University Press, 2022.
Identifiers: LCCN 2021051148| ISBN 9780810144651 (paperback)|
   ISBN 9780810144668 (ebook)
Subjects: BISAC: FICTION / Women| FICTION / General| LCGFT: Short stories.
Classification: LCC PS3615.B743 A78 2022| DDC 813.6—dc23/eng/20211019
LC record available at https://lccn.loc.gov/2021051148

For Ezra

CONTENTS

CHARLIE

I'm a little mystified when I hear about people who are friends with their college professors. They exist, these people, who correspond regularly with scholars decades older than they are, some famous in their fields. As students, they celebrated Thanksgiving at these professors' houses, house-sat for them whole summers, took care of their pets, their lawns, their kids. Years after graduation they invite them to their weddings.

How did these friendships form, I want to know. In college, as soon as class ended, I stuffed my books in my bag and got out of the lecture hall as fast as I could, assuming everyone else was doing the same. I never once went to office hours. People who loved office hours either had parents who were professors or were anxious about grades and wanted to ingratiate themselves, a personality type that disgusts me.

I was tipsily monologuing on this once, when a friend interrupted to say she'd always gone to office hours because she paid for her own college and wanted to get everything she could out of it. She wasn't trying to shame me, I don't think, but she did want me to shut the fuck up. My parents paid for my college, and I should be ashamed, because I treated this like it meant nothing.

I treated my body this way also, if that matters. I was the girl with puke down her dress the guy would send his buddy in to see after he'd had his turn. Back then it was important to me to show the world—a world certainly not paying attention—that I didn't give a fuck. This friend, the one who called me out, understood that enough to pity me, not hate me completely. But we haven't stayed close.

I'd been a precocious kid, queen of standardized tests. I ripped through elementary and high school hungry and angry, like, *Is that all you got?* Private school, Chicago. My parents and stepparents—all divorced by the day I graduated high school—were a doctor, two lawyers, and a management consultant. All four spoke constantly of scarcity, of stock market and real estate losses, precarity of bonuses, malpractice insurance. Tuition, Jesus Christ, the tuition. Once, checking out of a ski lodge in Steamboat, Colorado, my father turned to me and said, "You think it's nothing, don't you? Like everyone gets this, it's a God-given right. Look at this. Look."

He showed me the printed hotel bill, dot matrix strips down two sides of the paper. I was ten. The hotel had cost four thousand dollars for the week.

"That's just the rooms," he said. "Not the food, not the car. Not the thousand other things."

"Thank you," I said.

"You don't mean that," he said. "You're not grateful."

He was right.

The way envy works—I read this in *Scientific American Mind* at the orthodontist's office in eighth grade and it stuck with me always—the way envy works, you want as much of the envied thing as you can get, and whatever you can't get, you want to ruin. My mother and stepmother envied me for being a kid, no wrinkles, no cellulite, so they fixated on my prominent canine teeth, my acne, my eyebrows that grew together in the middle. No wonder I didn't have a boyfriend, they said. Most of the time I spent with them was at a salon or specialist, having hair ripped out or ironed flat, pimples injected with cortisone. We met once with a plastic surgeon I now see as one of the most responsible adults in my life, who told my stepmother my nose was still growing, it'd be a waste of money to do it now.

He looked at me with an expression I couldn't name. A combination of sadness and hope, telegraphing that the world was huge, life was long, that someday I'd be far away from these people.

Or I pretended he did. Sometimes I laugh at this fantasy and think this man probably had a daughter who disgusted him as much as I disgusted my parents.

So I'm a type, you know the type. You know the fun part: These parents of the violent caste are rarely around. From their unmonitored wallets I could steal a hundred dollars at a time. In their large, empty houses I could drink to blackout, have sex or masturbate for hours, cry at myself in the mirror. An older boy from another high school came over once and opened a package of prosciutto from my mother's fridge. He dangled a fatty pink piece in the air over his open mouth, but then changed his mind and draped it on my bare shoulder, beside the strap of my tank top.

"Ha, ha," I said. The meat was cold.

He peeled off a second piece and placed it on my other shoulder.

I'm thirty-eight now, married, have a kid, and I still masturbate thinking about this scene. In the fantasy, he pulls the straps of my tank top down over my arms, making sure the prosciutto doesn't fall off, pulls the tank top down and leaves it bunched around my waist. Then he pulls down my strapless bra and looks greedily at my nipples, which back then were soft and undefined. He puts a slice of prosciutto on one breast, then the other, and I loop the scene in my head—shoulder, shoulder, breast, breast—until I come.

In real life, he didn't pull down my tank top. Instead he opened the fridge again, and I remember clearly the contained smile that crossed his face when he got his next idea. He took out a pint of half-and-half.

"Can I pour this over your head?" he asked.

"Sure," I said.

I remember thinking he wouldn't really do it and also knowing for sure he would. He folded back the wings of the paper spout.

There was one professor I stayed in touch with after college. My last quarter of senior year, I did an independent study, because my friend who paid for her own college said I'd be stupid not to, it was the only way to get a letter. Until she said it, I had no notion of needing letters and at first thought "get a letter" was a Briticism for "get a good grade"—this friend had studied abroad and come back full of Briticisms. She marveled at rich kids, how we never thought ahead.

"My parents aren't rich," I said, because if there was one idea they'd beat into me, it was that.

"How much do they make?" she asked.

"I don't know."

"Uh-huh," she said.

She was right, of course, that I never thought ahead. That past summer, I'd blacked out and fucked some guy who somehow found my email address and wrote to tell me he had HIV.

I deleted his email, blocked him, and spent the rest of the day researching suicide methods, then cleared the cache on my mother's computer, which she yelled at me for later because it deleted all her passwords.

I got tested and was negative, but the nurse at Planned Parenthood said I had to retest in three months. For three months I spent most of my time immersed in suicide fantasies. I had a summer job making copies for an estate planner my mom knew from law school, and on breaks, I'd walk to Walgreens and stand in the pest control section, reading the copy on packages of rat poison, calculating how much larger a human was than a rat, how many poisoned biscuits I could ingest before vomiting. In three months, I tested negative again and wondered if the guy who emailed me had done it as a prank.

Anyway, my last quarter of college, in a late-breaking surge of entitlement, I emailed a creative writing professor and asked if she'd do an independent study with me. She said no, she was too busy, but then wrote again saying she'd found someone who would.

His name was Charlie. For ten weeks we met alone in his office, the door partly open. He read my short stories, full of long passages of dialogue between people screaming at each other about child support. In ballpoint in the margins, he wrote questions I knew were meant to be neutral but felt deeply personal—"What's the narrator's reaction here?"; "Should we have more of the daughter's presence?" Reading his questions moved me, which I knew was out of proportion, and I was often afraid to speak because I might start crying.

Who Charlie was, I barely noticed. He was on a one-year fellowship at the college, not technically a professor. He emailed me once to reschedule our meeting so he could fly to Nevada for a job interview, adding that he'd sure never pictured himself in Nevada. I asked no questions about this, including how it went or whether he got the job.

Based on a few things he mentioned, I calculated he was the same age as my father. I deemed it preferable to be my father—clean fingernails, good posture, the slightly starved look of a dedicated runner. Charlie was heavier, shaggier, much less carefully dressed. He had knee problems I had no idea what to say about, which he often brought up at the start of our meetings. At least twice he confused me with another student, who was apparently very into *The Sopranos*, then explained what was happening with the show's plot, apologizing but insisting it was important stuff for a writer to know. I waited, shy, almost mute, till it was time to talk about my writing.

Shortly before graduation, I ran into my worst ex at a bar off campus. I said hi, he said I looked like a whore, and I threw a drink in his face. Back in my room that night, quite drunk, I composed an email to Charlie describing the scene: rum and coke dripping down my ex's nose and chin, the little chip of ice that stuck in the neck of his T-shirt. His pathetic outrage, his friends dragging him away. "You need to leave," one of them said to me, and I just stared at him, thinking how much I wanted to try the palm strike I'd learned in women's self-defense, a hard jab from below that would supposedly break his nose. But all I did was stare, I said in my email to Charlie, and he backed the fuck off. I didn't leave. I ordered another drink, and the bartender said if those guys bothered me again let him know, and furthermore, I did not fuck the bartender. I hadn't fucked anyone in months.

Even drunk, I didn't send the email. I signed off, *Going insane but feeling incredible*, then cut and pasted it into a Word doc and deleted it from my email account.

A year or so later, I asked Charlie for a letter of recommendation for grad school. This was back when schools required paper letters, with signatures across the envelopes' seals, and as requested, Charlie sent me three. His return address was in Nevada.

I was living in San Francisco with Craigslist roommates, one who'd talked to me for hours in the kitchen one night after she had an abortion, who then moved out and I never saw again. My job was tutoring at a for-profit center for rich kids with learning disabilities. The kids criticized my accent and complexion, and spelled out *cock* and *cunt* with the alphabet tiles, openly curious what it would take to make me tattle. I didn't drink on the job but kept an airplane bottle of vodka in my backpack for the bus ride home each night, refilling it in the morning with a small funnel. Charlie's signature on the letters made me sentimental. It felt like a long time since I'd seen that handwriting.

I'd abandoned the idea of applying to grad school, so I slid my finger under the flap of one of the envelopes. The letter was nice. Between its lines I read true things: that I was talented but a little lost, that just a small amount of support would benefit me greatly. No one wanted to deal with someone like that, I knew. But Charlie meant well, and I wasn't offended.

A few weeks later, I stopped in a bookstore on my way home from work. I hadn't been inside a bookstore in a long time. Fifty milliliters of vodka wasn't much—most nights riding the bus I barely noticed a buzz—but walking into the store, I felt it. The lights were too bright, and I seemed to be moving faster than intended, gliding instead of taking individual steps. Impulses to do destructive things, like bite the books' smooth covers and leave teeth marks, kept floating up, delighting me and filling me with paranoia.

I found a rack of literary magazines and selected one to browse, laughing at myself for trying to pass as a casual reader of literary magazines. There, in the table of contents, I saw Charlie's name.

I read his story ready to be disappointed, to find him a boring, vain, middle-aged man. That was not what I found. I read the whole thing standing there, leaning on the magazine rack.

It was good. I don't want to summarize it. I was an idiot back then but was capable of real feelings. I don't have to prove that to anyone.

A couple years later, Charlie emailed to say he'd be in San Francisco for a few days and wondered if he could buy me a beer.

I was living with a man named Todd. He'd grown up in Alabama and saw this as something we had in common, both refugees from the Great Flyover. Chicago wasn't much like Alabama, I told him earnestly, and he laughed and said, no, of course. He was ten years older—I was twenty-five, he was thirty-five—and understood the world much better. His mother had died when he was in college, and the grandmother who'd helped raise him had died more recently, leaving him a small trust. It wasn't enough to live on forever, he said, but for now it kept him out of a cubicle.

His father, who hadn't been around much when Todd was a kid, was well-off now, remarried with two stepdaughters. They lived in the suburbs of Atlanta and were—Todd glanced theatrically from side to side, then lowered his voice to say the word—*Republicans*. Once a year his dad flew them all, including Todd, to Grand Cayman for a week, to pet stingrays and eat rum cake and avoid talking politics. "You might get to go too," Todd said to me. "If you're good."

Not long after we started dating, I said some insecure thing about how he'd probably decide I was frivolous and vapid, and he said the problem with women his age was they were mostly really bitter about men. Hearing this made me giddy with relief. It wasn't the compliment I'd been fishing for, of course. It was misogynist, and it made me feel less guilty about the two times I'd blacked out and had sex with other people. But it suggested my value was higher than I'd known, that he might not just be using me to kill time between real relationships.

I needed him badly. Even before I moved in, I slept at his apartment every night. The rare nights we spent apart I felt like I was going crazy, and to tamp down the craziness, I got drunk. Twice, I left mortifying messages on his answering machine. After that, any time I planned to drink alone, I hid my phone in an old purse on a high shelf in my closet.

All of this probably sounds horrible, but Todd was mostly very good to me, good for me. We went on hikes. We read *Harper's* in bed and saw art house movies and had a lot of sex, both of us always into it. When I got Charlie's email, I was using Todd's computer, sitting cross-legged at his desk in just my underpants while he made morning coffee.

"Aw," I said, as he set a cup in front of me. "My old professor."

He leaned over and kissed me. "You look so sexy like that," he said.

"He's going to be in town," I continued.

Todd turned the swivel chair so I was facing him and got on his knees so he could kiss my belly, slide my underwear down. Then he stood me up, bent me over his desk, and fucked me from behind. I stared into the multicolored fractals of his screen saver, the outline of my reflection in the black behind it.

"He's a really good writer," I said later, clothed, drinking coffee at the tiny folding table in the corner of his studio.

"You're going to hang out?"

"Yeah, it'll be fun. I haven't seen him in so long."

Todd moved around the kitchenette, just out of view from where I sat. I could hear him pour cereal into a bowl, open and close the refrigerator twice to take out and replace the milk. Then he came around the narrow wall that separated the kitchenette from the rest of the room and set the cereal in front of me.

"That's great," he said.

He was never jealous. At the beginning of our relationship, I worried he would be, and overexplained every male or lesbian friend. I told him how my college ex had read my diary and broken into my email, waited for me outside classrooms so he could scream at me about imaginary cheating. Real cheating also, but I didn't say that to Todd.

"Sugar," Todd had said, "I'm a grown-up."

My mother had been a year younger than Todd, I calculated, when she and my stepfather screamed at each other the entire two-hour drive from Inverness to some medieval Scottish castle about a restaurant receipt, a comment his sister-in-law had made, accusations about their architect—a blond woman named Carla who'd come to dinner several times—and counteraccusations about my mother's divorce lawyer, Terry, whose voice I knew from answering the house phone. I rode in back of the rental car, staring out the window at green hills, stone fences, sheep. ". . . would spread your legs anywhere," my stepfather said, and my mother lunged at him, and he shoved her against the passenger side window, splitting her lip, so that when she faced him again her teeth and chin were smeared with blood. These details were still bright in my memory. It was the day after my eleventh birthday.

"Do you want to meet him?" I asked Todd. He'd joined me at the table, with his own coffee mug and cereal bowl. The table was so small two cups and bowls were all that fit.

"Maybe," he said, taking a bite of cereal.

"I don't really know him."

"But you like his work?"

"This one piece."

It was the loneliness in that story, the vivid, specific loneliness, I'd been so moved by. I couldn't say that without sounding like a naive kid, romanticizing the loneliness of a self-absorbed academic. But I wasn't. There are a few things in my life I don't have to laugh at scornfully, and this is one. Anyway, the story wasn't about Charlie.

"What's it about?" Todd asked.

At some point, I'd made the mistake of trying to describe the story to a different guy, a friend's boyfriend who was in a PhD program, at some party. "See, the problem with American fiction," he'd said, and then talked for a long time. "Is that fair?" he asked when he was done.

Right then I remembered I'd once thrown a drink in someone's face, and the memory made me burst out laughing.

"What?" the guy asked.

I couldn't stop. My nose started running and I cried, "Holy shit," and wiped my nose with my wrist, my eyes with my fingers.

"You're really drunk," he said.

"It's hard to explain," I said to Todd now.

"Give me the basic plot."

He leaned over his bowl to take another bite of cereal. His hair, dirty blond and fine, stuck up in cowlicks all over his head, reminding me of a little kid's. He had crow's feet, and his lower teeth slumped to one side, so many years past being straightened. But bent over his bowl, in T-shirt and undies, he was like a large eight-year-old.

"What?" he asked, looking up.

"You're cute," I said.

He smiled. You don't even have a job, I felt like saying.

"Thanks, sugar," he said.

Charlie suggested a bar in North Beach, down an alley across from City Lights. It was a classic, he said, which Todd always said about places in San Francisco too.

Before I left work, I stopped in the bathroom to drink my tiny amount of vodka, brush my teeth, curl my eyelashes. I put my hair up, then took it down, put it up, took it down. I wanted to seem healthy, like I was doing well. Up, my hair looked a little greasy, holding the grooves where I combed it with my fingers, but down it was ratty, needed a trim.

It took me a minute to find the bar, its door shadowed by a fire escape directly above. Inside it was dim and nostalgic, plain wood tables, kitschy seafaring décor. Charlie was sitting at a table by the wall, a full pint of beer in front of him.

"Long time, no see," he said when I sat down.

His hair, which was still mostly black, had a little more white than I remembered, or maybe the white was easier to see because his hair was cut much shorter. He seemed to have lost weight too, and it occurred to me he cared more what the world thought of him than I'd always assumed. His voice was the same, though. Hearing it made me happy. It was weird, and good, to see him.

He got up to get me a beer—I said I'd have whatever he was having—and when he left the table, my excitement started to veer toward panic, as I realized I had no idea what to say to him. He hobbled a little walking to the bar, and I remembered his knee problems, but then thought it'd be awkward to ask about that. As he walked back, carrying my beer, I stared at the brick wall by our table, which was dense with framed photos, news clippings, display cases full of ephemera. We could talk about anything. The main thing was not to get too drunk.

He set the pint glass in front of me. "So how's writing?" he asked.

I blushed, then sat through the anxious aftermath of blushing, struggling, as blood drained out of my head, to be able to speak. He looked away for a second, as if something in the bar had caught his attention, and this left me with no doubt he'd seen me blush. I must have seemed young, ingenuous, possibly cutesy, none of which I wanted to seem.

"It's OK," I said over the alarm-like monotone sounding in my ears.

No one at that time in my life asked about my writing. I'd mentioned it to Todd when we first started dating, but now if he brought it up I felt like he was mocking me. But when Charlie asked, it was like he was giving me a compliment, and with my embarrassment I felt an outsized, soaring happiness that embarrassed me also.

"Good," he said, turning back to me like nothing had happened. "That means you're doing it."

"Well, sort of," I said.

"Right," he said. "I know all about sort of."

Then he talked for a while, like he used to in his office, about self-doubt and patience, how it was fine to be neurotic as long as it didn't stop you from working. His first year in Nevada, he didn't write at all, he said, but it felt good. It was the first time in his life he hadn't beat him himself up every day.

"I'm not kidding about every day," he said, looking directly at me.

"I know," I said.

"Every fucking day," he said. "No one should do that to themselves. Not even for art."

The last part seemed to be a joke, so I laughed, then drank what I was surprised to see was the last of my beer.

"But what if you feel terrible either way?" I asked. "Terrible, but at least you're writing, or terrible and you're not even doing that."

"Right, it's a dilemma." He finished his beer quickly, seeing mine was empty. "You want another?"

I said I'd get the next round, but he wouldn't let me. He got up, and I sat alone again, staring at the framed things on the wall. A restored photo of longshoremen on strike, stern-faced, wearing hats and smoking pipes. An old ad for women's face cream with the slogan *Unite against a common enemy*, a beautiful young woman squaring off against a haggard one. I felt wonderful. The beer had calmed me down but hadn't made me drunk, and I loved what Charlie was saying, and that he was saying it to me.

"I read a story of yours," I said halfway through the second beer.

"Uh-oh," he said. "Which one?"

I told him the title, told how it was the first time I'd ever picked up a literary magazine. "I loved it," I said, and then had to look down.

"I'm glad," he said.

I gathered myself to look up again, and when I did Charlie looked down, and I could see I'd made him happy.

"That character," I said.

"That poor guy," he said. "I didn't have to make him such a creep."

"No, he's perfect," I said, and I must have been starting to get drunk because I added, "It's exactly what loneliness does to you."

"Sure. To some people."

"Sorry, that sounds weird."

"Don't be sorry," he said. "But I do want to say—that charac-ter." He scooted his chair a little closer to the table. "I mean, he isn't me."

"Oh, no, I know," I said.

"I mean, I didn't—" He shook his head, his face serious. "I didn't rape anyone."

"No, of course."

"Always a great day when you have to say that, right?"

I smiled. "I knew he wasn't you."

"OK, phew."

He drank to the bottom of his beer, then pointed at mine, which had only an inch left. "Are we having one more? Or call-ing it a night?"

"One more," I said. "I'll let my boyfriend know I'll be late."

I'd gotten rid of my cell phone when I moved in with Todd, paranoid that having one aligned me with the rich tech people he hated, who were driving up rents, ruining the city. There was a pay phone back by the bathrooms, and when I picked up the heavy black receiver, I saw there was a condom stretched over the speaking end. It was unused, an anonymous joke I felt obliged to laugh at. I rolled the condom off the phone and car-ried it between my thumb and finger to the women's bathroom, where I dropped it in the trash and washed my hands. Then I needed to pee, and as I squatted above the toilet, the condom having made me germophobic, I thought about Charlie's story.

The character right away is bitter and defensive, addressing the world as if he knows its tricks and won't be taken in. He deals with loneliness and social awkwardness by trying to sanc-tify his solitude, like some kind of monk, when really he's a guy with a cube job, a crush on a coworker, who watches a ton of TV. He knows this, too—the cube, the crush, the TV embarrass him, as do his fantasies about solitude, which, when he comes out of them, he calls pathetic.

Reading it felt like reading about myself. The anger, which had no end, and the worthless ways I tried to give it dignity.

I wiped and flushed and thought of Charlie telling me he hadn't raped anyone. I washed my hands again. In the mirror I was much prettier now than before the beer.

I promised myself I wouldn't say anything else about the story. The woman the character rapes is someone who likes him, thinks he's just shy and that she can coax him out of his shell. They go on a date and afterward, back at her place, she wants to have sex with him. But it's pity, and when he turns violent it's like he's saying, *Here's what I think of your pity.*

I put quarters in the pay phone. The receiver smelled like latex—so stupid—and I was careful to hold it away from my mouth.

"Hey, sugar," I said when Todd answered.

"There was a condom on the pay phone," I said to Charlie, back at the table.

"Whoa," he said.

"Would it be OK," I asked, when the third and fourth beers were empty, "if I kissed you?"

Besides the bed, desk, and table in Todd's apartment, there was a futon folded into a couch. When I got home that night, I flung myself onto it, fully clothed, and passed out. I woke before dawn, rigid with panic, and got in the shower to stop my heart from racing. When I got out, Todd was up making coffee.

"Rough night?" he asked.

I left for work early and, on my way to the bus, stopped at a pay phone so I could call Charlie's hotel. He answered on the first ring and quickly apologized for keeping me out so late. I asked him if anything had happened.

"Oh," he said. "You don't remember."

We'd made out in front of the bar, then went to another bar, bummed cigarettes from these Goth kids, a detail that allowed him to chuckle, though I could tell he was nervous. Anyway, then he put me in a cab. "You got home OK?" he asked, and I said yes. I didn't ask what "made out" meant—probably it was minor, and anyway, I couldn't change it now. I said I should really quit drinking. He said he should too.

A few days later, I got on the computer in the break room at work and looked up Greyhound schedules to Nevada. The ride was ten hours. There'd be desert billboards, rest stop vending machines—for ten hours, loneliness would feel romantic. But I knew I wouldn't go. At best, I'd be an interesting nuisance, interrupting his work, running up his phone bill. We'd go out to eat and people would think he was my father, inverting what happened sometimes when I was with my real father and people thought I was his girlfriend. After a while, it'd feel textbook and embarrassing and I'd lash out at him because of that. At worst, he'd say he didn't mind.

I told Todd I was thinking of moving out. He said he understood—I was young, in a different place in life. He said I could take my time, look for a place, assess how I felt at the end of the month. I didn't mean we had to break up, I said, though that was what I'd meant originally. He shocked me by starting to cry, and I hugged him and said I still loved him. I thought about his dead mom, how he never talked about her, and said I wanted to quit drinking. He said he'd help me. Then, a few weeks later, I went out for a coworker's birthday and didn't come home at all.

After that, Todd cut me out completely. I had panic attacks for a few months, but gradually they stopped.

At some point during those months, Charlie sent me a long email. He said he was thinking about me and hoped I was doing well. Writing was going slowly, as always, but he was doing it. He hoped I was too.

Then he said he realized I didn't know much about him, and if it was OK, he wanted to fill me in a little. He used to be a really shy person, afraid to open up to people, and he was trying to do that more, open up.

His dad had walked out when he was three. His mom was a great person—he was amazed sometimes, thinking how hard she'd worked, holding down two jobs and taking care of him and his older brother, who weren't easy kids. His brother especially. Most of the email was about his brother, who'd beat up on him relentlessly the long hours their mother wasn't home.

It's not uncommon, Charlie wrote. Kids have nowhere to put their anger. He was still in touch with his brother, but it was hard to be close with him.

Anyway, he hoped it was OK to tell me that. He felt, for whatever reason, he should.

I was crashing with a coworker who was touchy about me using her computer, so I went to the public library to email Charlie back. There was a clock at the bottom of the screen that counted down the thirty minutes allowed for personal internet use. I reread Charlie's email slowly, then clicked reply.

Dear Charlie, I typed. *I understand.*

Then I stared at the screen until the clock ran out.

Charlie wrote to me once more after that, just checking in, he said. For months I planned to write back—*Sorry it's taken so long!*—and then too much time passed and I thought if I wrote now he'd tell me to fuck off, or that I didn't care about anyone but myself, or that I was too shallow to connect with anyone in a meaningful way. I thought all kinds of awful, true things he could say, and about how I'd respond, whether I'd fight back or tell him he was right or just block him. I also knew none of this made any sense. If I'd written back, what was much more likely was Charlie would've been nice to me. Then a bunch of other things happened, and I stopped thinking about it.

About a year ago, I googled Charlie and saw he was coming to Chicago to give a reading. I'd moved back before I had my kid, wanting to be closer to family, but both my parents ended up moving out west when they retired.

Charlie had changed his author photo and was completely gray now, with new, boxy glasses that looked good on him. I planned to go to the reading, but ended up getting in a huge fight with my husband and slamming out of the house without my purse. There was a fourth step meeting we sometimes went to at the Unitarian church on Damen, so I walked over and caught the second half, got updated on everyone's shitty bosses and exes and health problems. When it was my turn I just said I was grateful to be there, which is what you say when you're late and don't really deserve a turn.

Then I tried to walk to Charlie's reading. It was sixty blocks south and would have taken hours, but I walked that direction anyway, until I knew I was being stupid and turned around.

Maybe six months later, I googled him again and saw that he'd died. The funeral had been in Reno. He was sixty-three, survived by a brother. The obituary didn't give a cause of death.

I was home with my son, who was napping in my bed. Charlie died, I thought. He'd *died*. The fact of it filled me with a strange, bewildered lightness. If I met up with him now, over coffee instead of beer, the first thing I'd say was, "I can't believe you died!" and he'd laugh and say, "I know. What the fuck?" There was no one else I could tell, and I didn't mind knowing that. There are so many things you can't tell anyone, and that's just the truth, not a tragedy.

My son would be up soon. I was good with him. I did wish I could tell Charlie that, that I'd gotten my shit together to be good at that at least. My son wants me with him all the time. He's only three and can already write his name.

VALENTINE'S DAY

Maggie's mother still offered her a glass of wine every time they ate together.

When Maggie refused, her mother closed her eyes and nodded her disappointment.

"Don't you think by now . . ." she said.

"I can't," Maggie replied. "Pretend I'm allergic."

Her mother said drinking was not the problem. She often addressed this theory to restaurant staff.

"Her ex-boyfriend convinced her she's an alcoholic," she'd say, holding her wineglass by the bowl, agitating it. The waiter would wipe the neck of the bottle and pretend he hadn't heard. Maggie considered these moments a test of her strength.

"Well, anyway," her mother said at last. "She'll have a club soda. With a lime, right? Maggie? With a lime? Oh, come on."

In the beginning, Maggie promised herself she would stop eating with her mother, stop seeing her altogether. But she loved her mother. And she got lonely. Her sobriety books reminded her that life would always be difficult, and there were ways to embrace difficulty, turn it inside out. After a while, it felt strangely wonderful to be able to sit there, emotion pulsing like a tiny light deep in her brain, and to feel no flush burn her neck, no heartbeat fill her ears, no flutter of eyelids or clench in the groin.

Six months after she quit drinking, she also quit her job as a corporate accountant and accepted half the salary to work in fundraising at a women's health organization. Her new boss, Patricia, had a corona of black and gray hair, stark, dark eyebrows, and ice-blue eyes. She wore Navajo jewelry and carried a handbag printed with Van Gogh's *Starry Night*. From day one, Patricia called Maggie "Margaret," so everyone else in the office did too.

Though it forced her to move into a cheaper apartment, Maggie liked the new job. She liked Patricia and the younger, garrulous women in the office. At this time in her life, old friends seemed to be cycling out, having left Chicago for jobs in New York or Los Angeles, or husbands' jobs in those places, or to raise children in suburbs that could not be reached by public transit. Her new job seemed like it could replace all that, improve on it.

On her thirty-first birthday, Maggie relapsed when her new friends insisted on taking her out. She drank what she promised herself would be just one shot, some sort of cinnamon liqueur with gold flecks suspended in it. Later in the night, she remembered going to the ladies' and staring at herself in the mirror, taken aback by how beautiful she was. She'd posed shyly, as if she didn't want her reflection to think she was too vain. Electrified, heart knocking with the fear that someone would walk in and catch her, she planted her hands on the sides of the sink and leaned in to kiss her own lips. Then, embarrassed, she wiped away the faint spot from her breath.

She woke in the dark in her own bed, stripped to her underwear, at five A.M., and could not sleep again for worrying what had happened. At six she sat at the kitchen table, face bent over a cup of tea she didn't drink. She wanted to text the woman who had ordered the shots, Emily, her closest friend at work. But it was too early, and if Emily didn't reply right away, Maggie would have to wonder if Emily was disgusted with her or only sleeping. Finally, she put on her coat and went out to buy a bagel, which sat unwrapped but uneaten on the kitchen table until it was time to go to work.

She went to Emily's cubicle with tears in her eyes.

"You were fine," Emily swore, squeezing her arm. "Margaret, it was a fun night. Don't torture yourself."

Maggie went to a meeting that night, the only meeting she'd ever attended except for the day after Billy moved out. She didn't mind AA, she just forgot about it easily. At the meeting she cried again, but right away the tears felt stupid. They were unemotional, just a symptom of a hangover. At home she took a book from the plastic storage container under her bed and read the chapter on relapses until she fell asleep. She woke with hot lamplight on her face and a terrible pain in her stomach. All day she'd forgotten to eat.

Four days later, a man left her a voicemail. He called her Margaret and said he would like to see her again. At the end of the message he made some laughing reference to the song "Shelter from the Storm," and the ghost of a memory rattled in Maggie's head and made her mouth go dry. She hit delete. Then she blocked the man's phone number. Then she called her mother to see if she wanted to go to dinner.

For all her faults, her mother was a good talker. Listening to her, Maggie absentmindedly ate several rolls from the bread basket, then sat on her hands and tried to work seeds from her teeth with her tongue. Her mother's stories all took place at her law firm, and featured characters Maggie had not met but had known since childhood, like Paul Jackwin, her mother's nemesis, who was bitter that his department was run by a woman. Her mother's left eyelid drooped with sleep loss, and she occasionally dropped her train of thought to stare across the restaurant.

"Is that Matthew?" she asked suddenly. Her second ex-husband.

"That man's my age," Maggie said.

"Oh." Her mother pushed her crock of onion soup across the table. Its skin of cheese sagged into the liquid. "Here, finish that," she said, "I'm stuffed."

The meal passed without a mention of alcohol, but as they waited for the bill her mother said, "You seem depressed. Want me to make you an appointment with Allen?"

"I don't know," Maggie said. "I feel like if I'm going to see a therapist it should be a woman."

"Women shrinks are creepy," her mother said.

"Do I really seem depressed? I feel OK."

"Extremely," her mother said.

Life moved forward. A few months after Maggie's birthday, Emily took a job in Seattle. Good-bye was sad, but with that cubicle empty, Maggie felt relieved. It was as if whatever she had done drunk that night disappeared with Emily's dead fern, her box of Luna lemon bars, the smudgy digital print of a niece's first birthday. Emily left a picture of Gloria Steinem tacked up, along with a couple of feminist bumper stickers. After a few days, Maggie realized that those things had not belonged to Emily but to the person who'd had the cube before her, or before her, or before her.

Instead of an appointment with a therapist, Maggie's mother set her up on a date with an associate from her firm. Curtis was a talker, her mother said, but such a sweet guy. "He just moved here," she explained on the phone. "I'm afraid all he does is work. But he wants to get out, it's obvious." Here she paused. "He drinks," she continued. "Not a lot but, you know, normal. I was thinking you could just say you're allergic. Like you say sometimes."

Maggie did not say she was allergic. Curtis was much younger than she expected, which annoyed her immediately, though she knew that was unfair. She found him in the restaurant bar, halfway through his second Stella, and when the host came to take them to their table, he grabbed his backpack, with its Incase logo, from under the barstool. Her mother was his boss, he joked. He hoped he wouldn't do anything weird.

Maggie's irritation contained itself in a small place between the hemispheres of her brain. Seated across from Curtis, his forehead misted with sweat, she felt acute control of her face, each slow blink, each fluttering squint of misunderstanding. He switched to whisky and gave a long explanation of all the different kinds of whisky, and then told her why it made more sense to wait and buy a whole building instead of just one condo. When the check came Maggie quickly handed the server her credit card.

"Wait," Curtis said, moving to dig his wallet out of his backpack, but the server sided with Maggie.

"I insist," she said.

The next morning, Maggie took her first yoga class. The studio was on her walking route to and from the train, and for over a year she'd glanced in its windows, memorized its menu of prices, more than once took a flier and let it be buried in a pocket when she changed coats for the season. Sometimes on the way to the train she found herself walking behind one of the students, always a woman about Maggie's own age. At Lakewood and Bryn Mawr, this woman would veer into the yoga studio, and the timing worked out so that just as Maggie passed, the door swung shut, leaving her in a sprinkling of wind chimes.

"Don't look at anyone else," the teacher said at Maggie's first class. Sabine was her name, a fortyish German woman with yellow hair to her waist. She planted her feet on Maggie's rented mat and reached liberally for her thighs, demonstrating with both hands where to turn *out*, where to turn *in*. All class Sabine kept returning to Maggie. She took Maggie's rib cage firmly with her large hands, lifting it away from her hips, grazing Maggie's breasts with the indifference of a physician. In the mirror Maggie saw herself elongated, triumphant, a statue on a ship's prow, with Sabine's spread fingers girding her.

A new era began. Maggie felt cured. After work now she went straight to the studio, declining happy hour, declining her mother. Books on meditation, on Ayurveda and vegetarianism, replaced her sobriety books, and these she left in full view on her shelves. Soon her body began to change. She felt stronger, lighter, and because of this, less fearful. Small things, like replacing the water jug on the cooler at work or rearranging the furniture in her apartment, were easy now. And boredom and loneliness could be expelled by coming to the center of her newly cleared living room, planting her crown on the floor, and attempting, muscle by muscle, to raise her legs into a headstand.

"Yoga annoys me," Colin said the first time Maggie went out to tea with him. "It's cultural appropriation."

But this was now three years into her practice and she felt unshakable. She smiled forgivingly and said, "Everyone approaches it differently."

Colin looked at her for a long moment. His eyes moved systematically, up and down between her forehead and mouth. They were fleckless eyes, gray green and cloudy, almost like he had cataracts. He had a high forehead and a flap of side-parted dark hair going gray.

"I'm trying to think what you mean," he said finally. "You mean those who approach it approach it differently. Because surely not everyone approaches it."

Maggie pushed at her tea bag with the heel of her spoon, making it bleed rust brown along the white cup. There was a long crease across her forehead these days, and she briefly wondered if Colin noticed it when he studied her face. But not everything was a test. She let go of the spoon and bowed her head to stretch the back of her neck.

"It's not for everyone," she said.

She had met him at the Laundromat, the week before her landlady finally installed a coin-op machine in the basement of her building. She'd been reading *Walden*, a copy lent by a married man from the yoga studio. Colin had a lot to say about *Walden*. So much, in fact, that Maggie had stuffed the book back in her purse, her peace destroyed. Shortly afterward she saw him on the train platform at Bryn Mawr. He waved, and she waved back, and then she turned to look down the tracks to see if the train was coming. It was only a matter of time before they met again, this time at the big gardening store on Clark and Hollywood, and made a date.

He was handsome, and he didn't drink either, an AA veteran who'd tapered off meetings because he couldn't stand the religious stuff. Even the rational groups, he said, with their euphemisms like "universe." At the time, Maggie was troubled by her friendliness with the married man at yoga, so she tried to be open to Colin.

"Good," her mother said on the phone. Maggie now limited their meetings to once a month. "You need to get out more."

"Fresh air," Maggie said. "That's why I'm seeing him."

"I'm just saying it's nice to have dinner with someone. It doesn't have to be the love of your life."

"There's no such thing as the love of your life."

"Well, this is a pleasant conversation."

Maggie started to like Colin. He was serious, but he had a heart. And a year passed quickly.

On Valentine's Day, her boss handed around chocolate bars filled with vodka.

"If you eat it here, wait till the end of the day," Patricia said. She had a red gauze scarf knotted at her throat but was otherwise in black. Maggie thanked her and tucked the bar into the pocket of her coat. She waited until she got home to throw it in the trash.

She skipped yoga that night to meet Colin at an Italian restaurant down on Taylor Street. The only reservation he could get was early, so he drove straight from work and she took the Red Line train to the Halsted bus. She had put on makeup, something she rarely did anymore, and was a little excited by it, checking her face in the train window, fluffing her short hair with her fingers.

Colin wasn't at the restaurant when she arrived, so she waited just inside the door. It was an old-fashioned place, white tablecloths and candles, walls hung with still lifes of bread, bottles, and flowers in large gilded frames. Along the low ceiling ran shelves lined with casks, dark glass cased in straw. Almost every table was full, and those that weren't were set for two, burgundy napkins blooming from claret glasses. Soft accordion music, the theme from some movie, played over the loud murmur of the crowd and the clatter of ice from aluminum pitchers.

"One?" the hostess asked.

Maggie was startled. "Oh, no," she said. "I'm just early."

"What's the name?"

It took Maggie a moment to produce Colin's last name, Davis, a name so plain it almost asked to be forgotten. If she were Maggie Davis—Margaret Davis—but no, if she ever married, she would keep her own name. And Colin was not going to propose, and if he did, she did not know that she would say yes.

She gave the hostess her coat, then followed her back to the table, the very last in a tightly spaced row. Maggie squeezed in, her jacket brushing the vinegar cruet on the next table. A moment later, the waiter appeared and presented her neighbors' bottle of wine. They were a man and woman about her age, maybe a bit younger. Maggie watched the man receive the wine, watched him nod agreement with the bottle's label and avert his eyes as the waiter removed the cork. When the wine was poured, all three of them watched, the man, his date, and Maggie, as rich red liquid pooled in the oversized glass. As he tasted it, he caught Maggie staring, and she flicked her eyes away.

Colin arrived only a few minutes late. He wore a sport coat and tie, which he never did, and held three roses in green tissue. Before he gave her the flowers, he bent over to kiss her cheek. Maggie could tell that he had just smoked a cigarette. The man at the next table glanced over and saw the kiss, and Maggie was pleased. Now they were even. Colin sat down and handed her the roses.

"Happy Valentine's," he said.

"Is it snowing?" she asked.

"Just barely."

Colin's head was dappled with wet spots. When he'd kissed her, his face had been cold.

"Thank you for the flowers," she said. "That's so romantic."

The waiter brought menus. "Which of you likes to pick the wine?" he asked, holding up the list.

"We won't be having any," Colin said. He said it in the same tone he would have said, "I will, thank you." He was very good at this. Maggie pulled her napkin from her glass and smoothed it on her lap.

"No problem," the waiter said. "Would you care for Perrier, soda, ah, I believe we have orange juice."

Maggie imagined Colin ordering them tall glasses of orange juice, the two of them sipping it with their salads. She wanted to tell him this when the waiter was gone, tell it as a joke. But it wasn't that funny. The waiter took away their wineglasses.

Maggie laid the three roses along the edge of the table. Their stems reached more than halfway across, blossoms facing Colin. Through the tissue paper she could see the short tube of water attached to each stem. She touched one of the tubes with her fingertip. Then she saw that Colin was watching her, smiling.

"They live longer that way," he said.

Maggie pulled her hand into her lap.

Colin opened his menu. "I haven't been here in years," he said. "Do they still have Magdalena's special?"

"I don't see it."

"We should get it," he said. "Magdalena." He pointed at her to make sure she got it. Then he twitched his head to search the other side of the menu. "Maybe they've stopped doing it."

Colin had been married. Years ago, a decade. When he was still drinking. Maggie had not asked much about Kristen and tried not to let herself imagine anything. Land mines. That was how her mother described ex-wives. Maggie tried not to listen to her mother anymore, but occasional lessons presented themselves.

If she thought of Colin's ex-wife, it was in terms of a name, of phrases their friends would have said: Colin and Kristen are coming over, Colin and Kristen got engaged. The names went well together. Or maybe they sounded too similar. Without being told, Maggie understood that the end of the marriage had to do with Colin's drinking. Every addiction story followed one of a handful of scripts. She wouldn't have guessed Colin had cheated, like Maggie had done, but maybe he'd been violent. She watched his long-fingered hands tear a piece of bread. His old watch, with the beat-up leather band, slid up and down his wrist. Not violent, she didn't think. Not suicidal. More likely catatonic. And then she could see it, Colin in front of a much too loud television, chin reaching for his collar. A young man, but with this same haircut, dark haired and smooth faced and fully disconnected. No interest in sex.

"What are you doing?" he asked.

Only half noticing, Maggie had dipped her finger in the melted wax around the edge of their candle. The wax dried into a smooth, white moon.

"Taking fingerprints," she said. She pried the wax cap off her finger and dropped it back into the candle. "What should we get?"

With a dramatic burst, the waiter opened their bottle of *acqua minerale*. Colin asked about Magdalena's special, and when the waiter did not recognize it, Colin added that it would have been perfect, because of Maggie's name.

"Oh, OK," the waiter said, looking from Maggie to Colin. "I can ask the kitchen."

"No, no, no," Maggie said. A familiar embarrassment rose inside her.

They ordered, and then to change the subject she asked Colin if he wanted his gift. She prepared herself to receive no gift in return—the flowers, of course, were a gift, and all she wanted from him. "Here." She handed over a long white envelope with a heart drawn on the front in ballpoint. "It's stupid."

"Yoga," he said, looking inside. "You're trying to convert me."

"I think you'll be surprised," she said. "It's five classes. But if you hate it, they'll give the money back. I asked."

"I won't hate it," he said, sliding the certificate back into the envelope. Maggie could already see the envelope resting on his hall table, being slowly buried in junk mail. "I got you something too," he said.

The box surprised her, even scared her for a moment. It was small, covered in blue velvet, and had a clamshell hinge. Colin handed it across the table, smiling with his lips closed, looking shy. She wondered what he had done, almost asked him. Instead, she opened the box. It was a silver locket, delicate and polished almost to a mirror. Engraved in the center was the number five.

"It's beautiful," she said, lifting it out of the box. "What's five?"

"Years," he said. "Since you quit drinking. This March, right?"

"Oh," she said. "That's right. Good memory." She bent her head forward to clasp the locket behind her neck. "How does it look?"

Colin looked where the locket fell over her black sweater, at her sternum. "Really good," he said.

The man at the next table glanced over again. Later he and his date would talk in their car about the recovered alcoholics at the next table. Maggie turned her head slightly to see what the woman looked like, now feeling justified in looking. The woman had long hair that shone voluptuously in the candlelight. Without thinking, Maggie reached to her neck and twisted a piece of her own. So short. But she liked it that way.

She was glad when dinner was over. Outside the air was so cold it hurt to breathe. Snow clung to the mud where young trees were planted between sidewalk squares, frozen now, hard as the black sky. Maggie felt heat rush out of her body, into the vacuum of the cold, and the change made her giddy. She hunched under Colin's arm as they hurried to the car.

They walked past a bar, a dumpy little place with one small window high in the brick, too high to see in, opaque from the glare of its blue neon beer sign. It was the kind of place she would have gone in her twenties, with Billy, though they had both had the money to drink in nicer places. Maggie could see herself, talking loudly and making people laugh. All her books told her she only thought she was funny when drunk. It was the one thing she did not quite believe these five years. The circle of laughing faces, daring her to go up to someone and . . . The bartender chuckling that time she broke her heel and offered it in exchange for one last beer. "This is all I have," she'd said, holding out the red leather stump. The bartender pulled her a pint and said she owed him one. But it wasn't funny, what she'd done to Billy.

Colin opened the car door for her. She rarely rode in his car and its cigarette smell gave her a headache. Cold as it was, she cracked the window.

"Sorry," he said, "that thing doesn't help, does it?"

An air freshener shaped like a pine tree dangled from his rearview mirror.

"It's OK," she said.

They went to her apartment. It was too warm; the people downstairs were always asking the landlady to turn up the heat. She cleared some work papers from the kitchen table while Colin used the bathroom. She made tea, which went untouched, and they went to her bedroom. Colin kissed her neck, her breasts, and as she lay back, the chain of her new locket slithered along her lightly sweating skin. When his head was at her belly, she reached to adjust the chain so it wouldn't pull at her throat. He slid her underpants down and she rested a hand on his head, closing her eyes and letting her mind drift to something that would make her come. Billy. She could not think of the name of the man Billy had caught her cheating with; yes, she could, but didn't want to think about it. Shelter from the storm, she thought, and then the married man from yoga, she had never touched him. Then she pretended Colin was married and was cheating with her, then felt ashamed and tried to return to herself. Her body, here on the bed. She had never been so lean, so strong. Nothing, then, if she could just think of nothing. She arched her back to pull him up, moaned as he began to move inside her. When she came she made a noise like sobbing.

Colin didn't usually spend the night at her place. She was missing too many things, contact lens solution, morning coffee. He had trouble sleeping, and she suspected that he had a prescription, something he took only occasionally but liked to have on hand. What would he do if they ever got married? But she didn't know why that would make any difference. So many things were easy to hide.

Nude in the bed, she watched him dress, and thought of asking him to stay but didn't. He moved slowly, looking up at her from his shirt buttons and smiling, perhaps wondering if he should offer to stay, perhaps wanting to. She smiled back. He cared about her, she knew. It was all right.

Still naked, she walked him to the door. She hid behind the door when she opened it so no one could see her from the hall. Cold air from the hall prickled over her skin. Colin stood in front of the wallpaper in his coat, and glancing around nervously, he poked his head back in to kiss her one last time. "Happy Valentine's," he said, before she shut the door.

She knew she wouldn't be able to sleep. To relax, she unrolled her yoga mat on the floor near the radiator in her bedroom and lay on her back, drawing her legs into bound angle pose, feet together, knees butterflied. Each breath drew her closer to stillness, farther from the hard wood that grazed the outsides of her knees, the dust smell down here, the radiator's intermittent clanking. Air touched her body, and then her body was the air, and there was no discomfort, nor comfort, only being. Except she'd forgotten to lock the apartment door. The thought nearly slipped away, but then she imagined someone coming in. Her here, naked, prostrate. Her mother said a single woman was crazy not to have an alarm system.

Once up, she no longer wanted to be on the floor. It seemed silly. She went to the kitchen and poured the tea down the sink, flipped open the garbage can, threw the tea bags in. The vodka chocolate bar Patricia had given her lay there on top of the trash, not quite mingled with it. Out of curiosity, Maggie picked it up, wiping a wet spot from the label. She flipped it over and read the contents. The alcohol was nothing, practically nothing. She unwrapped it and broke it in half. The center was wet, thin as water, and it dripped on the counter. Half over before it started, she thought. It smelled like vodka, that was true. That clean smell, the smell of nothing. She broke off a small piece and put it in her mouth.

It was a good combination. The alcohol removed the excessive sweetness of the chocolate. She pressed it between her tongue and the roof of her mouth, sucking until it melted. It left the spots it had touched slightly numb. She chewed the next bite but didn't like the way it liquefied and clung to her teeth. She felt a little high, but this was implausible, probably imaginary. Still she closed her eyes and swayed her head a little, had one more bite and threw the rest away. This time she reached into the garbage to bury it. She put the tea bags directly on the chocolate, then pushed the whole thing down.

She washed her hands and made her way to bed. When she lay down, she realized her heart was pounding. She arranged her body in child's pose: face down, knees up to her chest, one cheek on the pillow. Then she took the pillow away and rested her cheek flat on the mattress, letting her neck release. Again, the new locket tugged.

She reached up and traced the chain with her fingers until she found the pendant. She felt its smoothness and the grooves of the engraving, and then she pulled it up to her face. The chain was just long enough to reach her lips. She put the locket in her mouth and held it there. It should have tasted like something, like metal, but it had no taste at all.

# #

Begin: *If I were a painter.* Because on the hotel bed, I'm naked but wish to be *nude*, painterly-vague and literal. *Nude* number something, a high number suggesting how many tries it takes to focus a moment. *A moment* is only a figure of speech, and I wish to be more than one numbered *Nude*, to be a series, numbers that increase by no discernible function. *#24, #41, #89.* Numbers suggesting final dissatisfaction with each try, suggesting temporary abandonment, effort applied elsewhere. Applied to objects—an egg, a photo of my mother when she was young, my own hand. But then a return. To me, here, *nude* on this bed. Numbers suggesting an abiding and fraught interest in this subject. For a time, if not a lifetime.

Naked on the hotel bed I asked my husband to take my photo. I've actually never been photographed naked, except once six months before this photo, when I was enormously pregnant. Then as now, I asked my husband to take the photo with my phone. In neither case did he ask to have or see the photo again. This is just an observation, I don't think I feel very much about it—my husband is attracted to me, I don't need him to want these photos. But because he doesn't, they're mine only. I'm alone in them, and no one else looks.

Naked on the hotel bed, I've just had surgery to remove a lime-sized malignant tumor from my leg. It's also my thirty-fifth birthday. With the tumor went the whole of my right rectus femoris muscle and a little of the two adjacent muscles. Thirty-three stitches, dark blue nylon, close the incision. At its base, just above my knee, there's a small hole where my surgical drain, a few feet of clear plastic tubing with a bulb at one end to collect fluid, is inserted. The fluid is pink, mostly water, some blood. I have a pamphlet on how to strip the drain—to "milk" it, the nurse said—to clear out tissue and to measure, twice a day, the amount of fluid that collects. The suction when I milk it isn't painful but sometimes creates uncomfortable pressure. But most of the nerves there are dead. There hasn't been much pain. Because of this, I accidentally tore away a patch of skin when I pulled off the tape and gauze the first time I showered after surgery, and in the photograph you can see the raw patch, an inch or so from the incision.

The final biopsy confirmed the cancer was low-grade and there were no cancer cells in the wide margin of tissue surrounding the tumor. In the photograph, I know this. The scare is over, and my body's only slightly changed.

Cloying, a high-art cliché: *Self-portrait with surgical drain.* I apply this title anyway, only in my mind, as I look at the photo later, embarrassed, delighted. The hotel bed's ivory-leather headboard is dimpled with grommets, glare to the right of them, shadow to the left. The reverse is true of my body's convexities, glare left, shadow right. If I were a painter, this pattern might rise to accidental meaning, though I'd want it meaningless.

What was there is what I'd paint, nothing else. Or so I believe. But I don't know anything about painting, just like I don't know anything about medicine.

What does *composition* mean exactly? In the photo I face the camera, lean back on my hands with my legs extended in front of me. Since childhood, I've had joint hypermobility—I can, for example, pull my shoulder out of joint and wrap my arm completely around my head, a trick I used to do for attention as a kid. In the photo my elbows are locked, my wrists hyperextended, hands turned backward, shoulders drawn up almost to my ears, creating a weird, monocular vision suggesting my arms have been torn off and sewn on again backward in their sockets. But the eye corrects for perspective. Looking at the photo I'm at first enamored of this quality, then not sure it's there at all.

Why not just *Untitled*: so sweetly permissive and passive, unfocused, uncertain? Right before the photo was taken, my son, not quite six months old, fell asleep nursing. He's out of the frame, dreaming prelinguistic dreams in the hotel crib. It'll be a few weeks of physical therapy before I'm allowed to lift him, so when he wakes to nurse in the night, my husband has to bring him to me. The day the doctor told me I had cancer, my husband cried and I didn't. Neither of us has since. There's been no reason. My son cries in the night but stops immediately when he nurses. He falls asleep again and my husband puts him back in his crib.

Before surgery, I hooked up my electric breast pump to collect one last bottle of milk before anesthesia, but because I'd been fasting since midnight my blood pressure dipped too low and I had to stop. The nurse put glucose in my IV and we waited half an hour for my blood pressure to rise to normal. After surgery I ate ice until they let me drink a milkshake. Then I pumped again and left bottles of narcotic milk on the tray by my bed for someone else—I don't remember who—to pour down the sink. In the photo my breasts are mismatched: the right nipple pale and elongated from being nursed, the right breast deflated; the left nipple flatter but the breast full, lumpy where the ducts are swollen. Faint but visible is pregnancy's vertical linea nigra, still bisecting my stomach from just above the navel to the top of my pubic hair. It makes a cross with the line left by my underpants' elastic.

This cross on my abdomen—I think, Christian cross, I think, crosshairs. I think, nah. Only a body. Or if anything, the cross is a more complex character, including the short flat line of my navel and the creases in my belly because of the way I'm sitting. I browse symbols in Word to see if one matches—I consider the euro, consider the yen, the less-than-or-equal, the approximately-equal.

If I were a painter, would I fixate as I do now on Pollock's having said, *No chaos?* Years ago, I read this in a curator's note. New York, the best hospital. As far as we know. The hotel's expensive, my mother is paying. In photos from now, I will someday seem young to my son. A general now, I mean, not the breathiness of *a moment.* The surgeon told us, translating the final pathology, that there should be plenty of years.

Lamplight flatters, my face is abstracted, glare left, shadow right. Dark eyebrow, light cheekbone, dark nostril, light white of one eye. Overview of the bedsheets, their wrinkles and puckers mountains on a globe. Mountains as shallow as braille.

SAVANT

She was small. Twenty-nine years old, she stood five feet two with her shoes off, so they were never off.

"Should I wear a ring?" she asked Nicholas when they went to meet with the real estate agent in the state, some Midwestern state, where he'd been told he should buy cheap properties to rent.

"Why would you?" he asked.

"Because people care about these things," she said. "These kinds of people care."

Nicholas cared about very little. No, that couldn't be further from the truth: Nicholas cared about many things, but few of them were visible. Of the visible, he cared primarily about his mother, his sister, and her, Sasha.

She followed him as he followed the real estate agent over the warped hardwood floors of a neglected bungalow. She attended to the sound of her own high-heeled boots attacking the boards and to the cold, skeptical mask she intended her face to be. She knew nothing about real estate. What she knew about architecture concerned cathedrals in Rheims and Tournai. But they shouldn't appear credulous. There was an ironic way in which a pair of artists from Los Angeles might be cast as naïfs in the mean little microcosm of small-town Michigan. One must attend to structural complexities. One must be aware.

In one of the bedrooms, there was a violent gash in the plaster.

"So, yeah, there'd be some work," the real estate agent said. She was Sasha's age, maybe younger, and she talked like a teenager.

Nick bent at the waist and peered into the hole. He was a tall, wide-shouldered man, and when he was unsure of himself his movements became affected, as now, hands joined behind his back, feet splayed in dancer's first position.

"That's fascinating," he said, looking at Sasha.

"It's something we'll take into consideration," she said evenly.

"You should look," he said. "It's fascinating."

He was giving them away. He did this also when he was unsure of himself, fixated on the symbolic resonance of some meaningless thing, excluding whoever else might be present. He was making them look foolish, but to even hint at this in words would only make things worse. She tucked her hair behind her ear. She looked at him impassively, did not speak, did not so much as glance at the real estate agent.

He straightened and folded his arms across his chest. A playful smile came through the frown he was directing at the hole.

"What do you think happened?" he asked the real estate agent.

"I honestly don't know," the girl said in her heavy Midwestern accent.

"But you must imagine these things. Did it happen while the owners lived here? Lovers driven to violence? Were there children?"

This was good. He was disarming her, looking into her milkmaid face and talking about something obliquely intimate, giving subtle sexual cues but none that could be called offensive. It worked on people—women—certain kinds especially.

The real estate agent looked away. "Yeah, I just don't know," she said. She turned back quickly, not to Nicholas but to Sasha, with a kind of pleading in her large mascaraed eyes. "I represent the seller, and in this case that's the bank."

Sasha stared at her. There was nothing *icy* about her stare. There was nothing cliché. It was the straightforward sort of look one human gave another before there was trust between them. But it, too, was disarming to people like this girl, who expected automatic sympathy. More than expected, they felt entitled to it. Sasha had never understood this.

"Of course," Nick was saying. "But doesn't it make you curious?"

"Oh, you see a lot of strange things," the girl said, "believe me."

Believe me, Sasha thought.

It was her money they were investing. Her money they had lived on, almost exclusively, the last three years. Her grandmother had left her a certain amount. She'd waited a year to tell him how much, which offended him, he said, but also made him respect her more. Still, it may have been the wrong choice to wait. When she finally told him, he seemed disappointed, not at the amount but at her irresolution.

Her heels made a different sound on the kitchen floor. Linoleum, the word, had meant nothing to her until now, as she crossed the large black-and-white checks, suppressing the urge to invent a superstition—white is quicksand, black are stumps. She watched the pointed black toes of her boots come down one after the other, small and precise and powerful, like occult fetish objects, crushing the seams between the squares.

"So of course you'd need to replace the fixtures," the agent said.

Nicholas crossed the room to look more closely at the sink. Passing, he moved so swiftly and so near the agent's body that she stumbled back a step and murmured an apology. Sasha was uncertain whether he did this intentionally. He liked to assert himself physically. He liked to violate puritanical conventions about personal space, about the separation of men and women. But also people made him nervous, and this probably explained his lurching and jostling better than any conscious philosophy.

He touched the stub of raw pipe where the faucet had been removed.

"Pillage," he said. "It amazes me that there are markets where these things can be sold."

"Oh, yeah," the agent said. "You should see some of these places. This one is actually in excellent condition. You still have pulls on the cupboards, most of the original glass windows."

He strolled along the counter, surveying the cupboards as if making crucial judgments about them. The agent took another step back and hugged her folder. Sasha was becoming impatient. To amuse herself, she wrote a mental description of the agent, from Nick's perspective. Pretty eyes—knobby chin—large, flat behind. But he would be more inventive than that. *She had the large, flat ass of a woman who spent most of her time driving between small Midwestern cities in a hatchback with a lemon-lime soda from a fast-food franchise jammed in the cup holder, ice rattling.* But he would be more succinct than that. *She had a large, flat ass into which her husband liked to sink his teeth.* And then, *She wore a large status diamond of inferior cut, which she cleaned every evening with a tiny nylon brush.*

Nick's phone sounded from his pocket. A single ring, like a glissando on a piano's top octave. He excused himself to take it, going out to the hall beyond the kitchen, leaving Sasha alone. To avoid speaking with the agent, she wandered to the kitchen window and looked out, in which compass direction she had no idea. Above the neighbor's roof the bare, axonal branches of anonymous trees swayed against the blue. It was his mother on the phone. He was asking about her tests. There was nothing wrong with her, but every few months she liked to make him worry. Languid smoke rippled out of a strange appendage on the neighbor's chimney, performing a veil dance in the air.

"So are you from California too?" the agent asked.

Sasha turned only her profile.

"It's interesting, the way you talk," she said to a love knot in the wallpaper's print. "You begin every sentence with 'so.'"

She turned back to the window. The girl would not ask her any more questions.

"Mama, promise me you'll take care of yourself," he was saying in the hall. "It's all I've ever asked of you."

Then he bragged a little about the investment he was working on. The window had been cleaned on the inside but was murky on the other, and in it Sasha could clearly see her own face projected onto the neighbor's ugly house. Contained as a classical statue, that face. There had been many periods in history when arrogance was a virtue. Behind her the real estate agent was pretending to organize the papers in her folder, blinking her big bovine eyes in confusion. Who *were* these people? she was surely asking herself, and Sasha was pleased to have raised the question. She did not aspire to be the sort of person about whom it could be answered simply.

They drove back to Chicago that evening, down around the wide trough of the lake and up again. Nicholas lectured her on economics. His father had been to Harvard Business School, a fact to which Nick had a shifting relationship. Today he treated it like an inherited trait.

"You're still not understanding," he said. "The repairs aren't our problem. We hire a management company to deal with all that."

"But how much does that cost?" she said, following with her eyes a distant shape on the roadside, fur, an animal, dead—but then they were past it and she hadn't been able to tell what it was. Raccoon-like but not raccoon. He would know.

"What that costs," he said, "is, in the larger context of this, such a trifling amount you'd laugh till you cried about letting it prevent you from acting."

"Act now!" she mocked him, in the husky voice of a radio ad.

"Ach," he said. "Don't do that. You're too good at it."

She was pleased. She played with the buttons in the car door until she'd reclined her seat halfway.

"Look at you," he said tenderly, glancing away from the road. "Who are you, Cleopatra?"

She closed her eyes. "Yes," she said.

"If Cleopatra were an imp."

"I'm an imp," she said, smiling.

"You're a perfect imp," he said. "An imp in her basket. That's your basket, it's made of reeds."

He meant the neutral color of the rental car's upholstery. She stroked it with both hands.

"I like reeds," she said.

She knew he was right. He had told her the parable of the two economists: Walking down the sidewalk, both see a hundred-dollar bill, but neither picks it up. Why? Because neither believes it exists. If it did, someone else would've picked it up already. He had spoken to her father on the phone for over an hour last week, and when he passed the phone back to her, her father had said, "That's a smart boy you've found, Ladybug. He takes good care of you."

She was self-aware enough to know her objections were only a feint, a way to keep the power balanced. Her money was not enough to live on forever, and his novel was both too radical and too sophisticated for them to dream of living on the sales. Her poems sold for nothing; she wrote them and gave them away as if blowing soap bubbles from a wand. They were undeluded—the relationship between talent and earnings was tremendously volatile. Nick's literary agent, who'd called his book a work of real American genius, had said from the beginning this might mean he'd never sell it.

Eyes closed, she attended to the car's gentle rocking as they skimmed over irregularities in the road. Even the words *real American genius* had a smarmy, disposable feel. There were no English words for what he was. He was extreme along a metaphysical axis. One had to know physics, religions, to say what he was. If there were a word, it contained silent consonants, primal vowels. And this—creature, creation, self-creation, presence— would not live with a woman only for her money. The thought was profane. She burned it in a tiny ritual fire behind her forehead. She was a baby devil tucked in a reed basket. The peasants had told him to pour boiling water over her, but he couldn't bring himself to do it, he'd fallen in love with her sleeping face, and so he brought her home instead to be his bride. He was watching her now, she knew, watching the dusk deal flashes of pink and gold across her silent, simple, child-lovely face.

His phone was ringing. She opened her eyes.

"Can you?" he asked, lifting his arm. She reached into his jacket pocket.

"It's she," she said.

"Answer."

The phone was silent after the first ring, but the screen lit up with a photo Nicholas's mother had taken of the front door of their family home. Last time they visited, his mother had taken the photo and set it to appear when she called, and Nicholas said he didn't know how to change it back.

"Hello, Vanessa," Sasha said.

"Nicholas? Who's this?"

"It's Sasha."

"Nicholas? Can you hear me? I'm looking for my son, Nicholas."

The phone connection was perfectly clear. They were sixty miles from Chicago. She could hear Sasha perfectly, and she knew who she was.

"Nicholas is driving, Vanessa," she said. "He wants me to talk to you for him."

"Tell her that doctor's in San Rafael, not Corte Madera," he said.

"Is this a bad time to talk?" his mother asked. "I don't want to be a burden."

"Here." Sasha held the phone out to him.

"Mama, do you have the internet in front of you?" he asked. "Look up cell phone, driving laws, Michigan."

"We're in Indiana," Sasha said.

It would have pleased her to have a good relationship with his mother. They didn't use the word *love* often, sapped as it was of linguistic vitality. But she would have held dear, would have expanded inside of, a trusting connection with an older woman. Psychological analyses were generally banal and reductive, but if they were entirely without power to compel, the discipline would not exist. And so, yes, undeluded, Sasha could allow that her past had shaped itself around a certain void.

"Of course it was Sasha," he was saying. "No, that's how she always talks."

Outside over a width of dry, harvested field, a bird of prey made graceful circles. Some sort of hawk, smallish, brown, not beautiful though its flight pattern was. To what music would she set that, if she recorded it? Minor key, minimalist—a nothing moment, antisymbol.

"Maybe she's picked up a bit of a Michigan accent," he said. "She does that, she's good at it. Pattern recognition is one of her savantisms."

They passed the hawk before it plunged. They passed farms and preserved forests, then train yards and factories so foul smelling she closed the vents on the dashboard, and still Nicholas talked to his mother. She was intrigued by the machinery exposed in the factories' construction, ramps and shafts and holding tanks. Simple and obscure, mute and hemorrhaging smoke. It was a hundred years too late to think of them as beasts. What instead? Only flimsy metaphors presented themselves, as if the factories' fumes inhibited imagination. She put her hand on Nicholas's leg and turned her face toward him.

"Remember your creativity, Mama," he was saying. "You tell *yourself* the story."

She pinched him as hard as she could.

"Spite!" he cried, pushing her hand away. "Mama, wait just a minute."

He held the phone against his leg, near where she'd pinched.

"What was that?"

"I'm getting lonely," she said.

At the hotel in Chicago, the first thing they did was sleep. They were amused by the euphemism *sleep*, the brilliant nonsense of it. She slept energetically, with raw appetite, on top of him, goaded by the thumping of the faux-walnut headboard against the wall. On the other side of the wall she imagined a middle-aged couple just coming in, in tuxedo and furs, from the opera. Immediately they'd hear the unmistakable noise—Sasha began to moan now—and as the middle-aged couple unhooked themselves, suspenders, brassiere, they'd chuckle mildly but not look at each other. They would feel their age. They would feel the way the evening cold had soaked into the fibers of the mink. Had this already been written, had she read it somewhere? Or was she writing it now? It was too early for the opera to be over. There was only an empty room, a strand of pearls on the vanity, shimmering in the dark in blue-gold city light through the window sheers, to hear them. She rocked forward and pressed her small hands high on his chest in a fan just under his throat. He pulled her long hair over his face. It covered his eyes, filled his mouth.

But the pearls would've been put away, hidden from the maids, she thought afterward, standing nude at the window with the curtains open. Behind her he was on the hotel phone ordering ham-and-cheese sandwiches, french fries, red wine. If she stood here long enough, indifferently regarding the dark river and lit bridges, he would say something about her bottom, her hair. They'd met tonight, she pretended, in this hotel. She was the daughter of a wealthy man, his business partner, and had been sent to him almost as a gift, but not quite, because Papa adored her.

"Maria's moving back in with Mama," he said.

She turned quickly. He was looking at his phone.

"What?" she said. "What about the money we gave her?"

"What about it indeed," he said, tapping the screen.

"Did she—"

"She says she needs to get away from—him, we don't have to give him a name."

He was sitting up against the pillows with the white comforter drawn up to his waist. He'd put on his glasses.

"I'll have a talk with her," he said.

Sasha picked up her white hotel robe from the carpet and wrapped herself in it.

"How much was the food?" she asked.

"Don't get like this."

"Just tell me, I'm curious."

"I don't know," he said. "They don't tell you that. And don't forget, it was your idea to stay here."

He wasn't angry. He very rarely became angry.

"I'd found us a perfectly adequate place by the airport," he went on. "You said—"

"I know what I said."

He stopped talking. Beneath the overbearing rationality on his face she saw a flicker of hurt, which had been her intention but now made her sorry.

"I just—" she said, feeling a sudden pressure rise from her chest to her throat. "I don't want to feel—" Two parallel tears slipped from her eyes and two more quivered in her lashes, blurring his image, squeezing and bloating particles of lamplight.

"Poor one," he said, opening his arms.

Whimpering, she crossed to him and scrambled onto his lap. He held her and stroked her head.

"This robe's much too big for you," he said. "You look like some kind of child empress."

She laugh-sobbed, a hushed and vulnerable sound, and felt her tears wet the light hairs on his chest.

"I know you worry about Maria," he said. "She's not strong like you."

Crying felt too good for her to stop and correct him. He knew he was lying anyway.

"You won't have to worry," he said. "None of us will."

His novel was about Maria. The title for a long while had been *Risa*, the character's name, like a ship, he had said, his first ship. But then he'd decided this was too commonplace. There was no title for now, but he knew it would come, when he was in some half-dreaming state from hunger or heat or from watching the wild parrots that flew in formation over the roof of their apartment some evenings. He'd begun the book a long time before he knew Sasha.

"Michigan will change everything," he was saying. "We should be celebrating. We *are* celebrating. We're staying in this nice hotel."

She lifted her head from his chest so he could see her face. Child-lovely, the lashes darkened from crying.

"I want to have a wedding," she said.

He closed his mouth.

"Nothing legal," she said. "You know I don't care about that. But I want to have the ritual, invite my father—"

"What about your mother?" he asked quietly, turning his profile, staring past the electric sconce on his side of the bed.

"I don't know," she said. "Maybe her too. I'll decide."

"And the money?" he asked. "And our ambitions?"

"We'll have money. That's what you just said."

His face came alive again, as if he'd had a new idea. He looked at her tenderly.

"All right. When there's money, maybe we will."

"Not maybe. Promise me."

She was kneeling now, her head higher than his, her knees pressing through the quilted robe and feather blanket into his femurs.

"You're too heavy," he said, nudging her, almost lifting her, off him and plumping her down like a cat among the pillows.

"I want you to promise," she said.

But now, aggressive knocking at the door. He threw off the covers and went, naked, to look through the fish-eye.

"It's the food," he said, unlocking the deadbolt.

"Are you insane?" she cried. "Put something on!"

"I am." He wandered into the bathroom and after a moment came out with a towel around his waist. A hand towel, she realized, and though it covered the front of him adequately it gaped at the back where he held it by two corners in his fist.

"Nick!"

But he'd already opened the door and was politely receiving the stout, acne-scarred waiter. Nick was still wearing his glasses.

"What?" he said when the waiter had gone again. "I've scandalized you?"

He threw the towel toward her but it caught the air and landed in his empty place in the bed. He seated himself at the table where the waiter had set their covered plates of food, their wine in small carafes beside their glasses.

"This is tasteful," he said, twirling the stem of the red carnation that had come in a little glass. She couldn't tell if he was joking.

"You should've tipped him," she said.

He slipped the flower's stem between his third and fourth fingers, cupped the blossom in his palm. He knew she was right. His mother had raised him and his sister in near isolation, without television, without school until he was fifteen, and though he extolled the effects of this on his imagination, he was at times profoundly anxious about conventions he hadn't learned.

"It's extremely rude not to," she continued. "They make barely minimum wage."

He drew the carnation dripping from its vase. "Why didn't you?" he asked, placing the stem between his teeth.

"I like to think you can manage a few small tasks on your own."

He removed the carnation like a cigarette to speak.

"Don't get like this," he said. "When you're ugly you tempt me to be ugly."

Since the waiter had come, she'd held her robe clamped at the neck, cowling the plush up around her ears and chin like a fur. He removed the cover from his plate, threaded the flower's stem through the little steel loop that was the cover's handle, and poured out his wine, lengthening and shortening the dark stream.

"Come eat," he said without looking at her.

The robe dragged behind her as she crossed the floor, but he wouldn't now make jokes, would not speak affectionately of his child queen. He was eating his sandwich already, elbows high and broad, naked lap fig-leafed with his cloth napkin. It hurt her when he wouldn't look at her, but she knew it was only a bluff.

"I still want you to promise," she said when she'd taken her place across from him.

He looked past her head at the gleaming black window, perhaps at his image in it.

"And what," he said, then chewed, then drank, "will you do if I don't?"

"I won't invest," she said. "As it is, I'm afraid we're being foolish."

It was crucial that she remain imperious, though the vacancy of his face now and the steady, rhythmically chewing jaw were unsettling her. He knew how to pull himself far inward, leaving an exterior blank and dull as a mannequin.

"And then what will you do?" he asked.

"Anything I like," she said. "Marry someone."

"You're not answering my question," he said. He let his eyes drift to her, but then, as if what he saw weren't enough to keep his interest, back to the window. "I asked what will you *do*?"

"What will it matter to you?" she asked. "I'll be gone."

He smiled faintly. "You certainly will."

She lifted the cover from her plate. It was crucial to remain even-tempered. She should not have cried earlier. She'd given herself away.

"Who'll pay?" she asked simply, and delicately bit off a corner of her sandwich. "Who'll take care of them?"

He nodded at the window, as if someone were there advising him. His smile was private.

"Do you remember that woman?" he asked his image in the window. "The woman who showed us the house?"

She paused. This was one of his tactics, to derail her with a riddle. She would not have stood for it, except that she may have, with her last words, begun to be cruel.

"Not particularly," she said. "Besides her vowels. I see, you'll go live with her?"

"Did you notice her eyes?" he asked.

She poured her wine from the carafe to the glass. Two dark drops splashed back onto the sleeve of the white robe.

"Did you notice the room service waiter?" she asked. "He was handsome, I thought."

He looked at her finally. He saw something he liked, but it wasn't what she wanted him to like.

"I'm not joking," he said. "She had extremely striking eyes."

"She had striking makeup," Sasha said. "You're not equipped to understand these things."

He turned back to the window. "They were uncanny. In the true German sense of the word. Unhomelike. Otherworldly."

She washed bread from her molars with a mouthful of wine.

"You should call her," she said. "Her number's in the folder."

"Eyes that remind you of something," he went on. "Something you want but don't want to want."

"This wine is gaudy." But it was as if someone else said the words. She was slipping away from herself. When he looked again, there'd be only a heap of white plush, nested around a small, roundheaded wooden doll.

"It's not uncommon," he said. "That phenomenon. An unearthly radiance in an otherwise ordinary context. There should be a word for it."

He took a large, untroubled bite of his sandwich and leaned back to chew, hooking his arm around the back of his chair. She came as near as she could to matching his bite, but her mouth was too small. In it the cheese was rank and fatty.

"It won't serve her," he said after a minute. "You see what I mean?"

"No."

"It won't raise her out of the mire. She'll die an ordinary woman with extraordinary eyes. That will be her epithet, and for only the briefest moment will anyone remember even that."

"Enough," she said.

"Of what?"

"This food is bland. I'm going to see if the bathtub's any good."

In bare feet she stood taller than he, lounging like a satyr, crumbs on his chest. She took her wine with her as she stepped around his extended leg, following the almost imperceptible lines left in the carpet by the vacuum cleaner.

"Be careful in there," he called when she'd passed. "Don't drown."

ALL ROADS

If you prefer, we're not American. You, dangling from that tall chair, projecting your self-conscious youth out over the rooftop terrace, haven't come all the way to Rome to drink with Americans. Besides, it's considerably more effort to charm one's compatriots. So we won't be. We're not.

Come. Yes, you. Sit with us.

This is Chris. It's a dull name, she'd rather you called her Dace. Her mother was Dace. D-A-C-E, pronounced DOT-sah. Isn't that pretty? It's Latvian. Her mother was also, very pretty and Latvian. We've said if we have a little girl someday—but we've also said we don't want children. Among our regrets will be the lost opportunity to name someone.

Let it substitute, then, that tonight, Chris's name will be Dace. Suspending a literal sense of history, believe it was she, this woman here, this vision in candlelight, atavistic jazz notes riffling the tendrils of her hair, who as a child fled Brezhnev after her artist uncle was dragged to a mental asylum. All those repressed memories are hers, firsthand. All her odd qualities, their manifestations. Call her Dace tonight, I will too, and she'll answer to the name. If we do this, I promise you'll get what you want, though you pretend not to want it: a true tourist experience.

Good. Now look at her, look at Dace. Notice her makeup. It's too much, isn't it? On a woman so fair, a redhead. You, wearing no makeup, think she'd be prettier without. You're from California? Ah, Georgia. But you've lived a long time in California. Even before you lived there physically—and yes, I know which college you mean, though coyly you give only the name of the town—even before that, you lived in California, through your television, your magazines. Of course you agree; you're "well educated."

Why this makeup, you ask? Young one, it is for profound historical reasons. This makeup is a mask. The adult mask worn by a child never allowed to be a child. Her uncle is taken away, her uncle himself so bewilderingly, wonderfully childlike, and dear little Dace is told not to cry. It's a charm—tell a child not to cry and the child never grows. I mean literally, young American. Your people take Freud for a metaphor, and how could you not? The idea sells so many books. But in Latvia these things work literally. Tell a child not to cry and she literally won't grow, and to hide this, her shame, she must wear gobs of makeup. You should see our hotel bathroom, every flat surface mosaicked with bottles, with brushes, false eyelashes, wig stands. Not a cell of her genetic body is visible, young one. Believe this. You met Dace, and you'll tell the story as long as you live. Europe will disappoint you unless you're permitted to touch it, though you've been warned the gold leaf will come off on your hands.

"He's drunk," Dace says, meaning what? Meaning me! Ah, she's being polite. But I've no such excuse, I've had just one grappa. I despised it, it was like drinking hydrochloric acid, but tonight is our first night in Rome, here we are on the roof of this old, self-important hotel, enveloped in decadent views of the domes. Something in me wanted to say, in italics, with exclamation point, *una grappa!* Dace said to the waiter, "He hates grappa." In Italian she said it. With languages she's a savant, I a dunce. I overthink them, she says. The waiter gave me an exceptional look of contempt, which tickled me—it was just what I'd come for, I wanted to tell him. Instead, he and Dace had several exchanges. Then he barked at me—a bark it was, though quite musical—*grappa?* Something in me now wanted to say an English *yes*, meaning, *sucks to your auntie.* But don't let this mean I'm American.

Now Dace tells you tonight's in fact our last, not our first, night in Rome. I hear her behind me, I've left the table to stand at the railing and feel the sublime on my face. The night is just as we've asked it to be, a sky the blue of the neural behavior of a Benedictine monk fixing a silver prosthesis to the foot of a statue pilgrims' kisses have worn to a nub. Moon over the Pantheon. Marcus Agrippa, son of Lucius, consul for the third time, made this. Silently, I ask you to tell me the difference between one's first and one's last night in Rome. On which is a young American woman so many standard deviations right of median intelligence most likely to come to bed with a pair of rootless cosmopolitans she meets on a rooftop terrace her guidebook rates quadruple dollar signs? Is it with the first or the last of her money she'll pay? Or with sex? No. I apologize for that. It's an ugliness in me, not in you. I would never speak it aloud.

We'll pay *il conto*, of course. Dace will, it's her money. And we won't even invite you to our hotel. Your body I can have right here at the railing. Your belly and bottom, rounded in homage to Capitoline statues, your small, earnest breasts, which you've sunned on the balcony of the too-small apartment to which you're assigned. There's no hot water in the kitchen, you tell Dace. You've been washing dishes in the shower.

"Kirsten," you tell her, and put out your hand like a cowboy, elbow held up over the dishes of olives and nuts.

"You couldn't look less like a Kirsten," I say, coming back to the table.

"Maybe it's not my real name."

Dace looks at you like a teacher at a pet pupil. Remember, she was never permitted to cry. With her benignant, condescending smile, her skin shows how fragile it is under the makeup. The lines fork and refork, fine as if drawn with the point of a needle. They disappear easily, but someday they won't. Someday they will deepen, will intersect to bound tiny areas that one by one will flake off.

Your history is tedious. A boyfriend in San Francisco. You must want to humiliate him, there is no other reason you'd give him a name as silly as Drew. Drew what?

You ask if I intend to befriend him on—and here you use the common name of an internet fiefdom of which, through the stock market, I own an invisible fraction. It's Dace's money, but she lets me pour a little of it back and forth between test tubes.

No, I say, I'm asking what it is he drew. A map of his birthplace? An anatomical diagram of his mother? The Jack of Phalluses? A diaphanous curtain across a whore's window display?

"What's your name?" you ask. Wise little one you are. I'll have to keep my eye on you. You know, as Dace and I know, how to make them keep their eyes on us. What's my name? I like you very much. Invent it yourself.

"I don't know it either," Dace says.

The table is round, but we three make points of a triangle. Obtuse isosceles, a miniature Pantheon's pediment. The longest distance is between you and me, with Dace between us, the apex. I reach for the arm of her chair, drag myself close enough to kiss her, her neck, her ear, her mouth. I begin to climb into her chair, but she stops me, a hand on my chest.

"Aivars," she says. "Your name is Aivars."

Her uncle. It doesn't make sense. He of the single apocryphal photo, unbound leaf of lore. Aivars the Great never met baby Chrissy. But I—I'm American. Don't shatter, *cher* Kirsten. I'll love you, I'll love you, till Riga and Lafayette meet. That's right, Lafayette, Indiana, back home a-gaaaaain!

"Aivars," Dace says, flinching delicately. Perhaps I am singing aloud. "We're playing," she says. "You have to play, too."

But it's true, Lafayette. It's where I was born. I return once a year on a bus from Chicago. Along the highway, they've built a wind farm, truly terrifying hundred-foot white towers, monocular turbines whirling so slowly time seems to slow with them. A phalanx of these, monolithic at roadside, minuscule at horizon. *Prospettiva esagerata.* I ride the bus because at fourteen, on a smaller but parallel road, I collided my mother's truck head-on into the car of a couple with children. Only I was hurt; they sued and we paid. I've come to love airports because at security I'm forced to confess the steel pins in my hips and femurs, reset twice while my bones were still growing. Without airports, I think I'd forget. So on and so on. Contrary to what Dace tells you, I now take alcohol with great restraint, and I don't drive at all.

Aivars is spelled with an s, Dace tells you, an s not pronounced.

Once on the ride back, before the bus reached the wind farm, I saw one of these windmills being carried off on a trailer. It lay like the Dying Gaul on its side. Write me a bathetic little poem, won't you, Kirsten? Today, you tell us, you walked an hour and back to EUR from Trastevere. You slip off your slipper, show Dace your blisters, spots of blood under your Band-Aids. She's very impressed.

"My name's John," I say. "Johnny. Johnnycakes. Gianni *ven tardi.*"

You had some cockamamie—your word, pretty one—some maim-a-cocky, comma-cakey, Akaky Akakiemamie idea you'd walk to Mussolini's Square Colosseum. To write about it, you guess, but if the idea's first, the poem never follows. Wiseycakes, you're embarrassed but really you're pleased with yourself. "The Square Colosseum," you mock. Your writing's been bad here, you can't shed yourself. Do we, does Dace at least, know what you mean?

The return of the waiter, my foil, with his miserable eyebrows that meet in the middle. He takes our olive dish—pit-iful, I don't say, it's my own private happiness, smell of the tiniest fart. He puts down a new *porzione*. Piggies, pale green, glisten in the candlelight. Dace orders Campari to taper me. For herself, another White Soviet. For you, whatever you like.

In passable Italian, you tell him what you like. Your flirting is tasteful, exactly enough. Men, just like women, want to be seen.

I am good, I am quiet. When he's gone, I will tell you my name.

"Please give us a pen," I say just before he goes. Dace explains you're a poet, you're shy, he forgives us. A heavy hotel pen he gives you and you, when he's gone, give it me.

The Square Colosseum. The napkins are cloth, so you tear me a page from your book. Its pages aren't meant to be torn, Kirsten. Who will forgive you? Dace asks gentle, teacherly questions about your poems, and these lead to your childhood in Georgia, some acres, a con artist father escaped to Grand Cayman. Your mother, when she was younger than you, had a job at a hotel bar in Atlanta, at which she did nothing—you love this, inwardly you verge on tears tinctured with infantile lust—nothing but dive again and again into a swimming pool. Instead of a baby grand among the humid ferns, your long-legged mother jackknifes perpetually, *plashless as they swim*. Pool the blue of your still-in-flux infant iris. On the rag-edged book page I graffito *Ephesian Diana*.

Cigarette smoke from somewhere. Perhaps after all you should come to bed with us. Our hotel room is shameless, it alone is worth your trouble. Un-European enormous, the bathroom especially. Tub faucet the face of a river god. In the mosaic ceiling, a Roman slave's suicide. It can be between Dace and you, what takes place in that tub. I'm too drunk. I'll sit on the velvet stool and draw on my face with Dace's black makeup. Already, in a much further future, you stand behind an American lectern. Your cheekbones have come out and there's a pronounced white streak, about which you are vain, in your hair. Through attractive eyeglasses, shyly, you read from your book a poem *for Dace*. This overpriced terrace, moon, and the ancient stones you could've had free in the street. This loose-jointed, swollen-brained man changes chairs, lopsides the triangle again, puts his hand up the crocheted back of your blouse—but with a single syllable, Dace stops it.

"He's tired," she tells you. "We've been traveling a long time."

An enigmatic, understated last line, *n'est-ce pas?* Your audience, when it's certain you've finished, will grunt softly. Turning the page, you'll remember the thanatos heat of my hand. *And fastened to a dying animal*, you'll want them to hear, but won't really want it. Their stupidity is sacred, it's something you need. They breathe an air recirculated so often it'd hurt their lungs to stand, as you have stood, you believe, on mountaintops. You slip your thumb from under the turned page of your book, your second published, the only one you actually like, and regard the cloying good taste of its design. Painfully, you wonder if even you have breathed that air. That searing clean. Perhaps there was no *Dace*, in italics, to binocle with your prepositions. *To Dace, with Dace, in Dace.* Perhaps none of this, table, candle, teeth scraping olive meat from pit, ever was.

"Her name's Chris," I say aloud. "Her money's from toilets. Toilets all over Chicago bear her name."

"Aivars." She's firm. "I'm Dace. Chris is at school in Connecticut."

Isn't she good? She's trained as an actor. I almost believe her, but no, I remember first seeing her surname as a school-child in Lafayette, pale-dark blue letters tattooed at the bottom of the lifted toilet seat. Every school toilet, every urinal, until at seventeen I left home. And then the miracle: the letters made flesh. Against logos, the logo transubstantiated into a woman. A copy of a copy of one American decade's notion of bohemia—all those safety pins in sweet Chrissy's clothes!—but under this, yes, a flesh woman. Her head half-shaved, the pale blue of her scalp. Guilty about money. About money, Kirstenka—imagine! We were children once, too. "Art students." "New York."

"My Chrissy," I say. "I miss her."

"She'll be home tomorrow," Dace says.

"We won't let her marry him, will we?"

"Only if she wants to."

"He can't even drive."

"She has a driver."

"He's after the money."

"But so was I."

And so she was. Pietà made flesh, greedy for money from toilets. In cash Dace nested, she laid her one egg. She saved onionskins to dye the egg red, needles to etch it with wheat stalks and flowers. When it hatched and the little one flew, piece by piece she put the egg back together.

"Still," I say, "shouldn't she find someone handsome?"

"Aivars." A flutter of eyelashes thickened with pigment. "You've never even seen him."

"I don't have to."

"He's handsome," she says, dreaming out of her eyes, infatuated with her generosity.

"Untalented, though."

"Aivars," she says. Otherworldly, the way she is never impatient. "He's a genius."

Who are we, Kirsten? With everything innocent in you, you watch us. *This poem is also for Dace*, you read twenty years from now. *This one*, about the bleach spots in your sense of history, sunbeams redacting the tales told on cathedral ceilings. Restorers on scaffolds, attempting to rebrain the Renaissance. Your poetry will be terrible, I hope in the very best sense.

The waiter's wake, a series of wet circles clichéd into plump paper coasters, reminds me you must not get drunk. I won't permit you. When you stand at the lectern, you won't want to have been. At your age I too often was, Dace will tell you. Blazon me your Drew, Lady Kirsten. His bony feet under the blanket, his slim, hairy calves. The way his back broadens waist to shoulders like a river. Scapulae, vertebrae: riverbed stones. Though there's no pronounced line, the skin on his neck is darker than that on his back. Unlike you, he stays out of the sun. Drew what? An anguished breath? Muchel drunk once at your age, I went to bed with a man. For years I tormented myself over that. Americano, the male conceived so strictly. Marcus Agrippa, son of Lucius, would hear it as idle gossip. But soothe him now, Kirstenet. Fell your Drew facedown and run your pretty hand up his neck into his hair. Tonight he is forty-six years old.

So as not to touch you, I pick up the pen.

Grand Cayman.

I pass you the page.

You've played this. Accepting, you gaze the most obvious direction, over the Tiber and up into St. Peter's wide wedding skirts. My ballpoint Diana's a chaste bunch of *grappe.* My handwriting ugly. Curved over your school-desk elbow, your hair is still dark. Dace and I look at each other fondly. Drew, in our mutual fondness for you, closer to each other. In your third and last poem *for Dace,* your bandaged feet touch the hotel bathroom's heated floor. From a heated rack, a towel big as a blanket. Fine rift of blood in the froth from your toothpaste. Some struck-through lines about Carrara marble.

"What time is our taxi?" Dace asks. She knows the answer, is only reminding me.

"Let's stay. Another week."

Fine cracks in her face. For the first time, they bind a small shape, and there, only there, a fragment of white falls away. Under it, her real skin. A beauty mark only I'd notice, just above, almost touching, her neatly drawn eyebrow.

"Whatever you like," she says in Latvian.

But Kirsten. You at least, at last, are taking the tour you've imagined. *For Dace,* the area of table inside your cradled elbow fills with postcard-colored water. In it, someone has chartered a small fishing boat. You are all of precocious eleven, you know many things, such as that the greed you feel now will be permanent. To lure the allegedly docile stingrays, he's bought frozen strips of breaded chicken. You doubt and you trust him. Other boats, bigger boats, have dropped anchor. A few sunburned Brits stand, squealing, waist-deep on the sandbar. The water's clear and you see the rays now, fanbacks wider than your arms, prehistoric spear tails.

You change your mind about going in. An audible cry in your head, your own far-close voice: *I've changed my mind, I've changed my mind.* He dumps out the pieces of chicken. They're coming. Their backs are like stones and their eyes are like birds'.

"Too late," he tells you. He's teasing, he'd let you stay up on the boat, but you'd have to show him how afraid you are.

Waist-deep in the water, you tremble. They bump you, playful and harmless as well-treated dogs. Tonight, when you learn to eat squid, you'll remember their texture. They school to you, Kirsten. He watches you fondly. There are as many as he told you, more than you imagined.

NINE

My stepmother had been engaged twice before she met my father. Once was to a man named Steven who had been a sculptor, and Abby still had a sculpture he'd made for her. It was an arch of cast metal mounted on a white marble slab. Each base of the arch was rounded and cleft to suggest a woman bending over. The bigger base was her bottom, the smaller her breasts. The top of the arch was her exaggeratedly slender waist. She was naked, and bronze, and streaked with mineral green, and the white marble looked like water she was breaching from, or disappearing into.

"Why didn't you marry Steven?" I asked. I was nine.

"We were too different," she said in her soft voice.

I stared at the sculpture. Abby had brought it when she moved in with my father. It went in the room she called the parlor, with her white couch and rug and glass table. On the table was a glass bowl full of clear marbles. I reached into the bowl, plunging my hand under so the marbles covered it. But I did this gently, wanting Abby to see that I was not a destructive child. She watched and didn't say anything.

"This feels good," I said, then drew my hand away.

The parlor was a room for adults. I had been told this but wasn't sure what it meant, if I was allowed to enter but not to play, to look but not to touch, or—as seemed clear from the way Abby lingered when she found me there—if I should not go in the parlor at all. Ignorance of the law was no defense, I knew well from my parents, who were both lawyers. But Abby showed no sign of being angry. No sign that I could see.

"May I have a snack?" I asked, to break the long pause.

The custody was exactly half-and-half. Before Abby, I had spent Saturdays downtown at my father's firm. He would set me up in the thirty-fourth-floor kitchen, with legal pads, ballpoint pens, and highlighters in pink and blue. Yellow highlighter didn't show up on yellow paper. He warned me never to touch the orange spigot on the side of the coffee maker, which poured out boiling water. But I had tried it once and hadn't burned myself.

Now Abby stood in the doorway of the parlor, waiting for me to pass in front of her. I ran, I don't know why. Into the hall and halfway down, so that when I looked again there were several yards between us. "Can my snack be Thin Mints?" I asked breathlessly, bouncing on my toes. "Please?"

"How many have you had today?" she asked. White light came in from the west windows and made her a dark blue silhouette.

"None," I said.

I took a few steps forward so I could see her better. She was shutting the parlor door, which took a few tries because the catch had worn smooth. The door had twelve rectangular windows. One was missing its glass. The movers had broken it when they carried up Abby's furniture. But they didn't have to pay for it, my father had explained. Their customers signed a waiver. Otherwise they'd never make any money.

Abby let go of the glass doorknob, and the door clicked softly and opened again. With more patience than either of my parents would've had, she closed it again, turned the knob back, and let go even more gently. It opened again.

"A ghost," I said.

She smiled.

"Maybe it's Steven," I added. When she didn't answer, I said, "No. He's not dead." She still didn't answer. I should not have said Steven's name. I stopped talking, letting my words fade in the air like a bad smell. Abby turned the doorknob firmly and the latch finally took.

"Let's change your clothes," she said. "Then we'll have a snack."

My mother had dropped me off that morning. She was half an hour late. My father phoned shortly afterward and Abby said, "They were half an hour late." Abby needed to nap today because she'd had a long shift in the emergency room the night before. She put me on the phone with my father so he could tell me himself. He needed me to be independent today.

Abby sat on my bed and cut the tags off the new clothes she had bought me. I took off my turtleneck and stirrup pants and stood waiting in my underwear. She glanced at me and then quickly looked away.

"I'll give you some privacy," she said, and got up and closed the door.

Abby had laid out the clothes the way I was supposed to wear them. The collar of the blouse peeked over the neck of the sweater, and the skirt was on the bottom, like a deflated little body lying on the bed. I touched my chest and felt the hard bumps that had formed there. I only knew they were there because I could feel them. I didn't think anyone could see.

When I came out, Abby was waiting for me in the hall. "You look very pretty," she said. "Let's brush your hair."

I had forgotten to put my old clothes in the hamper, but Abby didn't get mad. She picked up the clothes, folded them, and put them in a shopping bag to be returned to my mother. I brushed my hair in front of the mirror, and Abby helped me put in some barrettes. When we were finished, she crouched down and put her face next to mine in the mirror.

"Perfect," she said.

In the mirror, I could stare at her face more openly than usual. My mother had asked me whether Abby had gotten plastic surgery on her nose. I'd said no. Now I looked at the nose and wondered. It was narrow and straight, and the tip looked like a separate piece, like the lid on a tube of toothpaste. I didn't think she would choose a nose like that if it were up to her.

"We have the same barrettes," I said.

"You're right," she said. "We're twins. When your dad gets home, he can take our picture."

Abby went with me to the kitchen. She put two Thin Mints on a plate and cut up an apple and poured me a glass of milk. I asked her to tell me again about the woman who'd come into the emergency room with all her eyebrows and eyelashes plucked out. She was a famous rich woman in the city, but Abby couldn't tell me her name. Doctors had to protect their patients' privacy. The woman had checked into the emergency room saying she was in terrible pain. She said her eyelashes were growing in the wrong direction, they were curling inward and scratching her eyes. But when Abby looked closely, she saw that the woman had no eyelashes at all, no eyebrows, and she was wearing a wig over close-cut hair. Abby told her to take off her wig. The woman lay down on the hospital bed. Abby leaned over her with tweezers and pretended to pluck. Really, she was only plucking the air in front of the woman's face. "Oh, thank you," the woman said. "That feels so much better."

"You weren't even doing anything," I said.

"She thought I was," Abby said. "That's what made her feel better."

"But how?" I asked.

"Remember I told you? Sometimes people only think they're sick."

"But why?"

"I need to nap for just a couple more hours," she said. "When I wake up, it'll be almost dinnertime and your dad will be on his way home."

"Wouldn't it hurt to pluck out all your eyelashes?" I asked, and tugged gently on one of my eyelids.

"Eat some of the apple," she said. "Just one slice."

I pulled my lips into my mouth and shook my head.

"You're going to let the whole thing go to waste?"

I widened my eyes and nodded up and down.

Abby smiled a little. To keep entertaining her, I started speaking through my closed lips. *I don't like green apples*, I hummed, trying to make the inflection clear though the sounds were unintelligible. I hopped up and pointed at a green dish towel to help her understand. I pointed at a red apple magnet on the fridge, and then at myself, and nodded and rubbed my stomach. She watched, still smiling faintly. When I pulled the magnet off the fridge, a photograph of her and my dad slipped to the floor. She followed it with her eyes. I grabbed it.

Abby and Da-ad, sitting in a tree, I sang, still with my mouth closed.

"Careful!" she said. She said it sharply, and I was surprised. Either of my parents would have reprimanded me much louder and much sooner, but Abby never raised her voice.

"Don't get fingerprints on it," she said, this time more gently.

I held out the photograph and she took it from me.

"Where were you?" I asked, pronouncing the words normally.

Abby rubbed the photo with the cuff of her shirt. "My parents' anniversary party," she said. "Last year."

"When did you break up with Steven?" I asked.

Abby put the picture back on the fridge. She arranged the apple magnet to one side so it didn't cover their faces. The apple was the same size as their heads, so now the picture looked like three across, two human faces and a red blank.

"I'm going to lie down," she said, pushing my apple slices into the garbage disposal.

I went to the TV room. This was where most of my father's furniture had ended up. The plaid couch that had been in the basement playroom of the old house, the bookshelves from the old living room. The TV rested on what used to be a nightstand in my parents' bedroom, now with the VCR on the floor between its legs and videotapes in the drawers. I put on *Annie*. We'd taped it a long time ago, and it still had my mother's handwriting on the label.

The first few seconds of the tape had caught the end of a commercial. Kids in winter coats flashed on the screen, one at a time, each saying, *York!* in their own happy way. I'd forgotten about them completely but remembered them instantly, and liked the way the memory clicked into place. I crawled up to the VCR and hit rewind. *York! York! York!* I thought I could remember my parents setting up to tape the show, my father behind the TV switching cables, my mother in her glasses reading the instructions.

Abby appeared in the doorway.

"Please turn that down," she said.

I pressed the volume button on the TV. We had lost the remote control.

"A little more," she said.

"Is that good?" I asked. The movie had begun. Aileen Quinn was singing in the window of the orphanage.

"I'm really tired, kiddo," Abby said. She had put a sweater over her blouse, and now she pulled it tight and huddled into it like she was sick.

I pressed the button again. The whir of tape inside the machine was louder than the movie. Aileen Quinn sounded like a gerbil.

"Why don't you sit on the couch?" Abby asked. "So you won't wrinkle your new clothes."

When I had done everything she wanted, she went back down the hall. I heard their bedroom door shut and stared miserably at the movie. Annie was in bed with Molly now, hugging her too hard and stroking her face in a way that had always made me uncomfortable. *There, there*, she said. Their cheeks and hands were so chubby they made my teeth clench. My shirt had come untucked and the waistband of the new skirt was itching me. I pulled it back and looked at the faint red mark it left on my stomach.

After Abby had been gone a little while, I went out into the hall. The light from the windows had turned yellow and made long shapes on the floor. A big centipede glided along the bottom edge of the wall and disappeared under the apartment's front door. My impulse was to run and tell Abby, knowing I would get in trouble for that, but knowing also that I could act upset enough to justify it. Later my father would say it was no excuse, and I would cry, and he'd say crying wasn't going to work. That's not the way to get attention.

The light caught the windows in the parlor door except for the one with the missing pane of glass. I bent to peer through the hole. Then I pulled back quickly to glance down the hall. No one was there.

The door opened on its own. It floated in a slow arc and softly bumped the edge of the white rug. My elbows jerked backward, and my hands went up as if to shield my face. It was funny, how my body did things without me even knowing. Steven's sculpture stood on its table in the corner. I wanted to look one more time, just look, not touch. I dropped my arms to my sides and held them stiff and straight as I went in, careful not to touch the doorframe or step on the rug.

From far away, the sculpture looked like nothing but an arch, a heavy black rainbow misshapen at its two ends. Even up close, the only obvious human part was the butt, the seam between the two halves, the way it widened out from the waist. The top half of the body was out of proportion, much smaller, with really only a hint of breasts. The texture was rougher than I'd thought, lumpy like a melted candle. Burned into one of her legs was the initial S.

I expected Abby to be there watching when I turned around. She wasn't. I lay down on the white couch, on my stomach with my face turned out. The glass bowl of marbles reminded me of fish eggs I had seen in a slideshow at school. Fish eggs you could squeeze until they burst.

I put my hand under the waist of my skirt and rubbed the place where it itched. My breath was a little wet on the cushion, so I pressed my mouth closed. Only a minute, I would stay only a minute. It would be like I was never there.

THE FATHERS

The men got drunk two nights before the wedding. It was a large party—both bride and groom were from large Midwestern families—and because the groom hadn't wanted strippers, their entertainment was limited to drinking, cigarettes, and the bride's brother's one-hitter, shaped and painted like a cigarette, which he filled a few times and offered around but mostly smoked himself.

They met at a pool hall on a strip of Milwaukee Avenue crowded with music clubs, martini bars. With brunch restaurants that tomorrow morning would be as mobbed as the nightspots were now. The streets were jammed with taxis and slick with a light summer rain.

When the rain had stopped, the bride's brother Michael walked half a block from the pool hall to smoke in the alley. He was twenty-seven years old and had a young daughter by his girlfriend, but when he was out in the city he felt free from them. The alley's pale bricks, blue dumpsters, and slatted wood porches were gleamingly familiar tonight. They gave him the good feeling of being from a place, this place, part of it.

"Give me your money," a man said, approaching from the sidewalk, and for a watery moment Michael didn't recognize his half brother.

"What's up," he said then. They hugged, Michael holding the one-hitter away so it wouldn't burn Patrick's shirt.

"Did you go in yet?" Patrick asked.

"We've been there a little while. You want this?"

"No, thanks."

"Oh, right." Michael tapped out the one-hitter on the wall behind him and put it in the pocket of his jeans.

Together, they walked out to the sidewalk. They had different fathers but looked very much alike. Patrick was six months from turning twenty-one, and when he went in the pool hall, he showed Michael's old driver's license as ID.

The groom's father and brother and friends stood loosely grouped toward the back of the large, dark room. Each held a pool cue and a pint glass of beer, as if these items had been handed out as props. Michael and Patrick went to the bar, which was mostly empty, and Michael ordered nine shots of whisky.

"Is Mike Katsaros coming?" Patrick asked as they waited.

"I thought he was," Michael said.

Mike Katsaros was their mother's boyfriend. They used his full name because both Michael's and Patrick's fathers were also named Mike.

"What about your dad?" Patrick asked.

"He is, definitely."

"Is that going to be weird? Those two together?"

"No." Michael handed the bartender two twenty-dollar bills. "And if it is, I'm sure they'll handle themselves."

Patrick's father had not been invited to the wedding. The bride was an anxious woman, and she'd overthought the decision not to invite him, then overexplained the decision to Patrick. It was a matter of numbers, first of all, of costs, and besides, there would already be tension between her own divorced parents. It was not at all that she had bad feelings toward her ex-stepfather, she said, but Patrick knew she was just saying that.

"Here, I have money," he said as Michael took the tray of small glasses.

"Forget it. Get the next one."

By now the groom's father had put quarters into the pool table and was racking the balls too precisely, turning each so its number faced up.

"That nine ball looks a little crooked, Dad," the groom's brother said.

"Jeez, and look at the twelve," the groom said.

"My motto," their father said with mock ceremony, "is excellence in all things."

"Except golf," the brother said.

"Except golf." And the men laughed insincerely but hopefully, and when Michael came around with shots, they were relieved.

"A toast," the groom's father began. "Oh, no, wait, there's Mike K."

The bride's mother's boyfriend was crossing the room, waving hello. He was twelve years younger than the bride's mother, and the groom's brothers, who had not met him, were curious how he'd look, though careful not to stare.

"How's it going," he said as he joined them. "Oh, we're toasting."

"Someone get Mike K. a shot," the groom's father said. He took out his wallet and seemed almost panicked about making sure Mike was included.

"Don't worry about me," Mike said.

"Dad, relax," the groom's brother said. "Michael's getting him one."

It was Patrick, not Michael, who'd gone to the bar, but no one corrected this.

"Here, Mike," the groom's father said, "take mine."

"You know, I'm OK," Mike said. "I'm not really a shot guy."

But no one allowed this. Patrick came back with a whisky of a color slightly different from the others.

"What'd you get?" Michael asked.

"Scotch."

Michael pretended to be impressed.

"What? I didn't know what to get."

"That's the good stuff, Michael," the groom's brother said.

"So this one's actually Patrick," Mike K. said. "Though I can see why you guessed Michael. In this family, those are the best odds."

"Exactly," the groom's father said. "It's got to be Mike or Michael. Except in the very odd case of Patrick here, whose parents really thought outside the box." Then he laughed and looked around to make sure this was all right.

"Sorry about that," the groom's brother said.

"No problem," Patrick said. "It's the big joke with us."

"All right, people," the groom's father said. "I thought we were having a toast."

The men lifted their glasses, angling away from the pool table so they wouldn't spill on the felt. In the light from the high-hanging lamp the glasses and liquor looked emblematic, like an advertisement, and Mike K. took a photo with his phone as the groom's father began to speak.

"A toast," he said, "to my son, Brian, who I'm so proud of, and to his beautiful almost-wife, Janie. And to our families getting to know each other, which has been awesome. And to all of Brian's good friends over the years, especially his brother, because

I think of these boys as not just brothers but friends too. And Michael and Patrick, you guys are all brothers now, which you'll see from being married because I really feel that way about my brothers-in-law too—"

"Short and sweet, Dad," Brian's brother said. "My arm's falling asleep."

His father laughed. "You'll soon see I am known throughout the land for my gift of the gab, as they say in North Dakota. But really, I just want to say I love my boys so much, and I love Janie, and I hope we all have a great night tonight."

"Cheers," Michael said.

The rest of the men murmured cheers after him, clinked, and drank. Then they set the glasses on the tray again, and Brian's brother chalked his cue and took a clean first shot to begin the game of pool. Michael looked appreciatively at these men, his family now in a way. He looked at his half brother, whose face was startlingly adult, though his hairstyle and clothes were still a college kid's. This part was good, after all the waste and worry that came with a wedding. The bringing together, the arranging of all these separate pieces into a whole that made its own kind of sense, for a few days at least.

"How's your dad?" he asked Patrick when they went out again for a cigarette. It was dark now, and the rain had stopped. Traffic on Milwaukee was at full saturation, young, well-dressed people shouting to each other from either side, trotting between cars to cross. Down the block the Blue Line train clattered out of the station.

"He's good," Patrick said. "I mean, like always. Working a lot."

"Drinking scotch."

"Actually he's been cutting down." Patrick looked at the tip of his cigarette, which was burning unevenly.

"No, I just figured—"

"That's why I ordered it. Yeah."

Michael stepped back to let a group of women pass. "Excuse us," he said.

"How's Lucy?" Patrick asked.

Michael held his cigarette in his mouth and reached for his phone. He tapped the screen a few times, then turned it so Patrick could see a photo of Lucy, almost two years old, splashing wildly in a plastic swimming pool.

"God, she looks like Meg." Patrick leaned to look but didn't touch the phone. "She's cute."

"She's obsessed with water," Michael said, turning the phone to look at it again.

"So now is everyone asking if you're going to get married?"

Michael didn't answer that. "Check it out," he said abruptly, and keeping his cigarette in his mouth, crossed the sidewalk, stepped off the curb, and opened the door of an idling taxi.

"What took you so long?" he asked, leaning in.

In the taxi, Michael's father was signing a credit card receipt against the vinyl seat back. Patrick flicked his unfinished cigarette into the street, briefly anxious about being seen smoking, though as soon as he did this he felt embarrassed. Mike Conlon was not his father, no authority over him, and look—Michael smoked in front of him. Still, he was glad not to be smoking when Mike Conlon climbed out of the taxi. Much of his life, Patrick had seen the man at a distance, through windows and doors. Sometimes Patrick had opened the front door for him and they'd waited together in the entry of Patrick's mother's house, on the red Turkish rug that Conlon once said was technically his. "It goddamn well isn't your rug," Patrick's mother had said, but Conlon had looked at Patrick and pointed at the rug and nodded. "Just get out," his mother had said then, "you can wait in the car." Patrick, though wordless through the exchange—he had been six, seven years old—had felt his mother's bitterness, and hurt for Mike Conlon, and heard in his head his own voice saying, *Stay.*

"Patrick," Conlon said to him now, coming close, folding a handshake into a half embrace.

"Good to see you," Patrick said.

"Man, I am—" Conlon began. "Linda and I had dinner with—" Some names Patrick didn't know. "And man, we got into the wine."

Michael laughed. "Perfect."

"I'm fine now, though," he said. "But about an hour ago I was feeling—but how's, what's going on in there? Is the party already over?"

Patrick followed them in, keeping a few steps behind, watching. For no reason at all, his heart had begun to pound, and he went only a few more yards with them, watching as Michael showed his father the phone picture of Lucy. Conlon held the phone away farsightedly and smiled. Patrick's tongue felt dry. He tried to tell them he was going to the bathroom but knew he hadn't been heard.

He passed the groom's father coming out of the men's room, and nodded an awkward hello. There was no one else in there, which was lucky. Patrick went into the stall and stood away from the toilet, which frothed with blue cleaning product. It made no sense that this was happening; he had not smoked pot in months. With his back to the toilet, he opened his wallet and pulled out a strip of foil-backed pill blisters. So far he'd used them only twice. Now, he pushed a third pill through the foil and tipped it from his palm to his mouth.

Out by the sinks again, he felt the likelihood of someone walking in, felt certain they would—and they could, it didn't matter. The psychiatrist had said it was common as ibuprofen. But no one came in the bathroom. At the mirror he saw no sign that his heart was pounding, though he still felt it and heard it. This is how I look to them, he thought, turning slightly to look at one side of his face, then the other. A lot like Michael, but no, like himself. He looked like himself.

The pool hall seemed darker now. Across the room the men were hard to tell apart, except in the light over the pool table, into which the groom's father now leaned to shoot. The place was filling up, blurring with unfamiliar men, women too, but more men. Drifting among them, Patrick felt separate, unseen. He saw Michael leaning into the bar, two fingers extended and lightly clasping a folded bill.

A few steps behind his son, Mike Conlon stood gazing vaguely at a baseball game on the high-mounted television. He was shorter than Michael, something Patrick hadn't noticed until now. He'd always been bald, and now his head was shaved perfectly smooth. Patrick remembered that when they were kids, Conlon had often come straight from the gym when he picked up Michael and Janie, still wearing a T-shirt and shorts. Had he meant to impress their mother? She had left him, had fallen in love with Patrick's father, though that had lasted only a few years. What had she given up in Mike Conlon? Patrick felt he might understand the man better, if—something. He didn't know what. Now Conlon's arms were crossed, his mouth slightly open, and his eyes lifted to the television, strangely wistful. Then the game cut to commercial and Conlon seemed about to turn his head, so Patrick looked away.

"Dude, he is wasted," Michael said a minute later, when Conlon had gone to say hello to the groom.

"Who, Brian?" Patrick asked.

"My dad."

"You think? He seemed OK to me."

"I mean, he's fine, he's just wasted," Michael said. "Look at him."

At the other end of the pool table, Conlon was gesturing toward Brian with his full pint glass. Beer slopped over the rim onto his sleeve, and Brian stepped back, laughing. Conlon widened his arms, frowned at his hand, cursed. Then he grinned at Brian and held out his dripping hand as if it were wounded.

When Conlon went to get napkins, Michael walked over to Brian, and Patrick followed.

"Did he spill on you?" Michael asked.

"He's hilarious," Brian said. He seemed fairly drunk himself.

From the other side of the room, Brian's father suddenly cried, "Yeah, baby!" Then he cocked his pool cue at his shoulder like a rifle and pretended to shoot.

"Sore winner," Brian's brother called through a cupped hand.

"Nobody likes 'em," Brian called back.

Brian's father leaned back on his heels, now playing the cue like an electric guitar.

"Good," Michael said. "He's having a good time."

"So, you're getting married," Patrick said to Brian. "Are you nervous?"

"I seriously don't even know anymore." Brian pushed his hair back with his palm. "I'm in some kind of protective cloud. Like all I can think about are small things, like who's picking up my grandma at the airport. I'm not even thinking about the wedding."

"Good," Michael said. "That sounds good to me."

"I mean, of course I'm thinking about it, but."

"No, I get it."

"What about you?" Brian asked. "Is all this making you think—or that's a stupid question."

Michael shook his head. "She's talking about it. I'm saying not yet."

"Sorry."

"No, no." Michael took a long sip of beer. When he finished, he said, "It's a legitimate question."

Brian poked with his straw at the ice in his cocktail glass, then moved the straw aside and drank what was left. "What about you, Patrick?" he asked. "Are you scoping out the bridesmaids?"

"The bridesmaids are old," Patrick said.

Brian and Michael laughed.

"Erin used to be hot," Michael said. "I haven't seen her for a while."

"No, they're hot, I'm just saying—"

"Erin's still hot," Brian said, "not to be—"

"Totally," Michael said.

At the other pool table they were racking a new game, and Mike Katsaros was pointing around, taking drink orders. He'd cuffed the sleeves of his lawyerly dress shirt and his hair was coming slightly out of shape. He grinned hazily as he headed toward Patrick.

"Who needs something?" he asked. "Guys, the groom's standing here with an empty glass."

"My bad," Michael said, "what was it, gin?"

"I'll get it," Katsaros said. "I was just kidding."

He glanced toward the bar then, and though the change in his expression was subtle and brief, all three of the boys noticed. Each found a way to see what he was looking at, though none made it obvious.

"So, gin?" he said, turning back.

"Here," Brian said, "let me give you some cash."

"Put your money away." Katsaros said. "Michael?" he said. "Patrick? You're sticking with beer?"

They watched him walk toward Mike Conlon, who was returning from the bar with a wad of white paper napkins in one hand, a beer in the other. As they passed, Mike Katsaros nodded and held up his hand in a motionless wave, and Mike Conlon lifted his elbows, looked at his full hands, and smiled helplessly. Then Conlon looked at the boys and raised his eyebrows and shoulders in a big theatrical gesture, beer tipping diagonal and nearly spilling again.

"Was that OK?" he asked, coming over.

"What?" Michael asked.

"Is this weird for you, Brian?" Behind his glasses, Conlon's eyes were shimmery, lids heavy.

"What, hanging out with you guys?" Brian asked.

"No, I mean, just, all these people from all these different times in your life," he said. "Is it kind of poignant? I mean not poignant but is it—God, am I being—am I just sappy?"

"Kind of," Michael said.

"No, I know what you mean," Brian said. "It's intense, it's—yeah, I don't know."

Michael had pulled out his phone. "Hey, I'll be right back," he said, and headed toward the door.

"I don't remember if I even had a bachelor party," Mike Conlon was saying. "Or is this the bachelor party? Is this just like the dads' get-together?"

"This is it," Brian said, chuckling. "Yeah, I didn't do the whole, you know. Traditional."

"It's nice that you wanted your dad here. He's great. He's a great guy."

"Oh, thanks. I'll tell him you said that."

"Tell him I said that."

Then Mike Conlon trained his eyes on something unseen and seemed to withdraw into his own smile. There was a long pause, filled with the noise of the bar, during which Patrick sensed faint lines connecting himself, his brother-in-law-to-be, his brother's father, a little triangle of charged space, into which you might've tossed an object and the object might float. Conlon was still holding the pile of napkins down at his side, a blank, flimsy hand of cards.

"But it's not like you guys had a bad childhood, right?" Conlon said suddenly, looking up at Patrick. "Lots of people loved you. It wasn't like with my dad—you know about my dad, right?"

"Sort of," Patrick said, though he didn't.

"Oh, my dad was," he said. "You know this, don't you, Brian?"

"Janie kind of told me," Brian said, gently but without being too serious. He folded his arms and leaned slightly forward, as if to hear better, or to keep Conlon from having to speak louder.

"All right, so you know." Conlon raised his glass but didn't drink, just held it near his chin and said nothing. Patrick waited. He resisted an impulse to look over at Brian, feeling that to do so would be like disrupting a coin in perfect spin, a plain disk turned briefly into an uncanny sphere. Conlon moved his glass away from his chin and looked at it as if recognizing it for the first time. Then he searched around for a place to set it down.

"Don't let me get sappy," he said, turning back. "I need to save that for the wedding. So are you excited, Brian? Or is it kind of weird? Just all these people."

"Hey," Brian said, because Mike Katsaros was standing near them now, three drinks bunched in his hands in cloverleaf formation.

"Sorry to interrupt," Katsaros said. "Just handing these over."

They took the drinks and thanked him. Visibly stiffened, with a huge but tight-lipped smile, Conlon stepped backward and dropped his head as if listening to a far-off sermon.

"This was supposed to be Michael's," Katsaros said. "Did you see where he went?"

Conlon looked up, raised his brows, and shook his head solemnly.

"I bet outside," Patrick said. "I bet he's on the phone with Meg."

"OK, well make sure he gets it. I've got a few more to pick up at the bar. Mike, you want anything?"

After a pause, Brian added, "Mike?"

"Oh, me?" Conlon looked like he'd been startled awake. "Oh, no, no, no. Sorry, I didn't realize."

Katsaros looked at Conlon. It was an expression Patrick had seen before, one Katsaros made when Patrick's mother was, as she often was, moody and demanding. It was an utterly neutral expression, its only trace of emotion a mild, attentive curiosity.

"Well, if anyone needs anything," Katsaros said, turning to Patrick. "You've got money?"

"Yeah, I'm good."

"OK, well let me know," he said, and before he walked away reached out to tap Patrick lightly on the arm. This was unlike him, and there was something sad about it.

Conlon watched him leave, craning so blatantly that it was like he wanted Katsaros to turn and see him.

"I'm sorry, but it still kind of freaks me out," Conlon said. "He's not still in his thirties, is he?"

"No, he's like forty, what?" Brian said, looking at Patrick. "Forty-three?"

"Something like that," Patrick said.

"I mean, seriously. Why would a guy that age—" Conlon picked up his beer again. "It's not like he needs her money. He's got money, right?"

"Yeah, who knows," Brian said. "Hey, so how's Linda?"

"I'm sorry," Conlon said.

"No, no."

"Patrick, am I being an ass?" he asked. "You're—Brian's not used to all this, is he?"

Brian chuckled. "Mike, don't worry about it."

"Hey, who said you could call me Mike?"

Conlon now seemed close to falling asleep on his feet. The glass in his hand was sliding downward in tiny increments, and Patrick prepared himself for it to plummet and smash, knowing that no one, himself included, would try to stop this from happening.

"So," Brian started to say, but then his brother was shouting his name. Across the room a couple of Brian's friends stood near their semi-abandoned game of pool, chatting with a dark-haired, dimpled cocktail waitress. Patrick saw that Michael was back there also, grinning and nodding as he listened to Brian's father, who was half-telling, half-acting a story that seemed to involve ogres or bears.

"I better go over there," Brian said.

"I'll go too," Conlon said, brightening suddenly. "Tell me your dad's name again."

As Patrick followed them, carrying Michael's full beer, he saw that his own glass was close to empty, that he'd been drinking faster than he thought. But he felt fine. He felt good. His pace across the bar floor, weaving between chairs and pillars and people, was frictionless but controlled so that, though just ahead of him Conlon kept stopping, they didn't collide. He didn't

mind how drunk Conlon was. Really, he kind of liked it. To ask
again about Conlon's father, that strange ancestor, not family but
not completely unconnected to Patrick, would be tactless. But
he wanted to know more. He felt he could map their lives, as in
the front flap of a book of myths, could set all the complexities
of marriage and parentage in a forked geometric diagram, if he
knew enough.

"Remember that, Brian?" Brian's father called.

Brian was standing awkwardly with the cocktail waitress
while his brother took his picture.

"He doesn't hear me," his father said.

"This is yours," Patrick said, handing Michael his beer.

Michael held out his hand for the glass. "Don, have you met
my dad?" he asked.

Having put the two fathers in conversation, Michael separated himself by a few steps, pulled out his phone, and tapped
the screen.

"Jesus motherfuck," he said, and then glanced at Brian's father
to make sure he hadn't heard. "Look at this." He showed Patrick
the phone. "Can you read that?"

Patrick read the screen, a sprawling, rancorous text message
riddled with typos. "Is she OK?" he asked.

"She's fine, she's just sitting home boozing while the baby's
in bed, getting all worked up for no fucking reason. Sorry."
Michael took the phone back, closed the message. "This isn't
your problem."

"That's annoying," Patrick said.

"Story of my life." Michael set his beer on the edge of the pool
table and began to rearrange his pockets, taking out his cigarettes, putting away his phone. "So what's been going on over
there?" he asked. "Is he about to pass out?"

"Nah, he's OK."

Michael turned his head and for a long moment looked at his father, though his hands kept moving, knocking then twisting a cigarette from his flattened, soft pack. Conlon was nodding along to what Brian's father was telling him, squinting and listing slightly forward, as if his upper body had become too heavy. But then Conlon said something, and both men laughed. They were fine. Michael put the cigarette behind his ear.

"You can have that beer," he said.

As Michael walked away, Meg's language expanded in his head, competing with his almost perfect certainty he'd done nothing wrong. The tamest bachelor party in kingdom come and she—ha, kingdom come, his mother's old phrase. The filthiest jeans in kingdom come, or the longest radio song, when mornings on the way to elementary school he'd made her listen to the hip-hop station. He'd write that to Meg—tamest bachelor—but no, he wouldn't write back at all. It was better not to give attention.

Along the sidewalk ropes had been put up around some of the doors, penning the waiting crowds. Michael leaned against the pool hall's windows. He felt himself being seen as he lit his cigarette and took out his phone to seem occupied. He opened Meg's message again and, hardly reading, smiled at it affectionately, pretending it contained a compliment, tender, understood only between two. He laughed a little as he scrolled. Tapped the reply field, pecked out the letters *I love you*, and sent.

The door swung open and Mike Katsaros emerged, holding it open for Brian's blinking father.

"He's hungry," Katsaros said when he saw Michael. "We might go grab a bite."

Brian's father peered up at the sign above the pool hall. "This is where we just were," he said.

"Flash Taco," Michael said, gesturing toward the end of the street. "Kitty-corner from the El." In his pocket, his phone pulsed.

"Great," Brian's father said. "That's great. Good idea."

"See you tomorrow," Katsaros said. He reached out to pat Michael on the shoulder, but Michael took it as a hug and leaned over, and for a second the two men stood side-by-side as if posed for a photograph.

"OK," Katsaros said. Brian's father had started down the sidewalk. "I better—"

"Yep," Michael said, taking out his phone again.

He had a message, not from Meg but Patrick: *You outside?* Mild guilt, he'd left his father in there grinding the gears of his psyche, stalling in fifty-year-old memory. His sister was this way too, a bad, sentimental drunk; he'd had to chase her around bars a few nights over the years before she quit altogether. *Yeah,* he texted Patrick. Not just sentimental, either. Angry sometimes. Once she'd cursed out a whole table of her friends, old friends— but enough. She was fine now, had found this Brian, who seemed like a good guy.

His phone pulsed in his hand. Meg.

You're an asshole.

Now the door swung open on his father, newly animated, talking fluently, Patrick following.

"Just whack, whack, whack," his father said, "and I had to, like—" He bent his knees slightly and covered his head with his arms. "Just shield myself till it finally quit."

The bouncer asked them to move, they were blocking the door.

"Sorry, sorry," his father said.

"How's everything going?" Michael asked.

"Good," Patrick said, "we're talking about the nuns."

"You remember my Sister Joseph story," Michael's father said. "Holy Spirit, third grade? Suzy Gorman's report on dysentery?"

Michael gave Patrick a cigarette. "Probably," he said. "Hey, where's Linda? Where are you staying tonight?"

"Can I have one of those?"

"Seriously?"

"Yeah, I used to smoke." His father smiled at him dreamily. "You don't know me, do you? You think I'm just some old man."

Michael laughed. "Not at all," he said.

"You'll see," his father said. "It happens to everyone. In your head you feel about twenty-one." He accepted the cigarette Michael held out for him and arranged it between two fingers. "And you know no one else sees that, and you don't even see it in the mirror anymore, and I tell you what. It freaks you out."

Michael flicked his lighter and his father leaned toward the long flame. He had trouble getting it lit at first, and then when he got a mouthful of smoke he let it all out immediately, without inhaling.

"When did you get married?" Patrick asked. "I mean, how old were you?"

"Twenty-one," he said. "Think about that. I was your age. When I was Michael's age I had two kids."

"Trippy," Michael said, but not quite mockingly. His phone went off again.

"Hey, don't do that," his father said. "Be here. Talk to us."

"Can't," Michael said, opening the message. Another long screen from Meg, this time a sort of apology. *It scares me that I sais something like that to some I love more than life or even my own child.*

"It's Meg," Patrick said.

"Oh." Michael's father looked at his son with a brief, pained expression, then fell quiet, gazed out into the street.

"Same old bull shhhark," Michael said, putting the phone away, smiling lightly. "She's fine."

"Your mother was the same way," his father said, sipping at his cigarette like a straw. "Both your mother. You know what I'm talking about, Patrick."

"Bitches be crazy," Michael said.

"No, I'm serious." His father turned his head to see who was behind him. Only strangers, only the bouncer. "I wouldn't say it to Brian," he said, turning back, "but marriage isn't—" He shook his head. "It's nothing like you think."

"I know," Michael said, not joking now. He felt a sudden gentleness toward his father. He did know, he wanted to tell his father. It was nothing like you think.

"And the kids," his father said, looking at them searchingly.

"Do you think—" Patrick began.

"It'll hurt you is all I'm saying. You recover, you have to, but it will. What, Patrick?" he asked. "What were you saying?"

"I was just asking," Patrick said. "I mean, I know the story, about how you and my mom split up and everything."

Mike Conlon nodded his head solemnly. The cigarette burned in his loose hand, forgotten.

"And I just wondered. If there was any way you were actually my dad."

Michael's throat tightened. He watched his father, who lifted his lowered head and smiled sadly, but also with something opposite sadness. There was this good thing about the man. He could look straight on at a moment like this.

"Patrick, I would be honored," he said. "To have you as my son—that would have been—I would be honored."

Patrick listened, his expression unchanging.

"From what I know," Conlon went on, "from what was going on at that time, I'm pretty sure your father is your father."

"I mean, I guess I knew that," Patrick said. "But just cause of everything that happened, I just wondered."

"I used to think about it," Conlon said. "I used to wonder, but I guess I knew—"

"No, I know."

For a moment, all three were quiet and stood banked against the wall, out of the stream of passing strangers. An urge came over Michael to put his arm around his brother, who looked shyly at the ground, flicked the filter end of his cigarette, smiled a little, raised it to his lips. He could have. Could have embraced his brother, slid out on the drunken unfurling of feeling, but if he did, this strangeness still would follow, and *it* was what was really happening. How could he say—it was their strangeness to each other—all of them. His father sleeping with eyes open behind his glasses, crying-laughing with eyes dry—his father smoking delicately, squinting, the cigarette perfectly centered in the O of his lips. Without deciding to, Michael put a hand on both their shoulders.

"Let's go in," he said. "I'm going to buy us all a drink."

He came in upset, Michael's stepmother told him later. Slurring badly, saying he'd been in a fight. But with the lights on she saw he was unharmed, his shirt untucked but clean. A young guy, half his age, he'd said, and he'd won, he'd kicked his ass. Had anything happened, Linda asked. Not that he knew of, Michael said. They'd put him in a cab around one, definitely drunk but not at all angry. He was so angry, Linda said. He kept talking about beating someone up, and she kept asking him, who, who?

And then he—Michael, he started crying. She'd never seen him like that in her life, he was crying so hard, and he wouldn't say why. Finally she just put him to bed.

Michael didn't know. They'd had one last drink, Patrick's choice, Irish whisky, and then went back to swim among the tables with the laughing brothers and friends and strangers. Mike Conlon was given someone's phone to take a picture of Brian with his brother and Patrick and Michael, four in a row, glasses raised. He should be getting back, he said after that. They took him outside, and Michael hailed the cab himself and told and retold the cabbie the hotel cross streets. He'd made sure his father had enough to pay.

Soon after that the rest of the party got hungry and shoved off for the fog lights of Flash Taco. But Michael and Patrick stayed out shooting pool and were kings of the table for some time before they were back on the blue-lit sidewalk, then back in Michael's dark apartment, trying not to wake the baby. They'd made it home some way, though that last hour was gone from his memory. But everyone had made it home.

THE DEAL

Here was the deal: Carol would pay for her son to go to law school if he enrolled no later than the fall of next year. She would give William an apartment in one of her buildings in Logan Square—she knew from being in real estate that all the hip young people wanted Logan Square. They wanted Humboldt Park if they were broke, but William was not, not with her patronage.

Free tuition, free rent, and a negotiable monthly allowance, on the condition that he complete his degree by age twenty-six. Carol didn't tell William her real feelings about this deal: that it was ridiculously generous, that at his age she'd have killed for an opportunity like this. When he told her he'd have to think about it, she told him to take his time. She was a businesswoman. She was even a little proud of him for playing coy.

Built into the deal were fifteen straight months, between William's graduation and the start of law school, during which he would study for and take the admission test, complete the applications, and wait. Nothing else would be expected of him during this time. If he liked, he could work for Carol, get some experience, save some cash. If he'd rather, he could go to Yellow-stone, where his friend Daniel was a park ranger. He could live with Dan, work odd jobs, write songs for the guitar, take his skis to the Tetons on weekends. The year off was an incentive. Carol believed in incentives.

The summer after graduation, William moved home for a few weeks and slept in his old bedroom but did not unpack his boxes. He left his duffel bag open on the bedroom floor and took clothes out only as he wore them. He did his own laundry, as he always had growing up. One morning, as Carol stood at the kitchen window smoking a joint with her coffee, a young woman in a sundress came tiptoeing down the front stairs and slipped out the door.

"Was that Katie Murphy up in your bedroom last night?" she asked him that evening at the restaurant.

William gave a guilty smile. He said he didn't know what she was talking about.

"That's funny. I could've sworn a girl came down while I was on my way out to work. Maybe I was hallucinating."

"It wasn't Katie," he said. "At this point, you can rest assured that Katie won't be coming over."

"But it's someone I know?"

The waitress put down their plates, filet for Carol, the vege-tarian option for William. She asked if he wanted another Jack and Coke and he said yes.

"I don't think I want to tell you," he said. "It's not a serious thing."

Carol was amused. She was in love with her son, and this sort of conversation made her want to flirt with him, which embarrassed him and propelled him away from her. So instead she gave a theatrical shrug.

"It's your business," she said.

Then she asked, "Whatever happened to Katie, anyway?"

"Why does it matter?" he asked.

But after a minute he told her Katie was in Uganda with the Peace Corps and had a serious boyfriend from Chapel Hill. William didn't really talk to her anymore. She wanted to be friends but he didn't.

"Well, that's too bad."

"It isn't too bad," he said. "That's the part that's so hard for you to understand. People go where they're going to go. Life is unpredictable. That's what I love about it."

"I see your point," she said.

I see your point—magic words Carol had learned much too late. With William's father and in the relationships that followed, at work and during the years William was a teenager, these words could have brought so many better outcomes. But she had not known how to be strategic back then. She had relied on a lot of wrong assumptions about how people worked.

In July, William packed his car for Yellowstone. Carol sat on the front steps in a blazer and skirt, bare legged and wearing pointed pumps that showed cleavage between her toes. She fanned herself with a folder of listings. Her clients were picking her up today because their four-year-old needed a car seat and Carol's car didn't have one. She had come close to telling the clients that a four-year-old didn't need a car seat. But not too close. Air conditioning streamed out the open door of the house, keeping her from sweating too much in her suit. William disapproved of this, but Carol insisted. She couldn't be sweaty when her clients arrived, and she wasn't going to watch through glass while he drove away and left her.

"You're right," he said. "Since this is the last time I'll see you for the rest of my life, I guess we can make an exception."

"Don't joke," she said. "You don't know what's going to happen."

Two days earlier, Carol had transferred five thousand dollars into William's account. That was to last him the summer. She told him if he couldn't make it last the summer, she would know he was on drugs. He said it would last much longer than summer, and that once he got a job he would send her a check for whatever was left. He refrained from getting touchy about the implied accusation, which was groundless and Carol knew it. He refrained because six months earlier Carol's friend's son had taken too much ecstasy in Tulum and died of dehydration. Now that woman's life was ruined. Ruined. "Fucked," Carol had said, and William had said, "I know," and she had said, "No, you don't."

Now he clamped his skis to the rack on top of his car.

"There won't be snow till November," she said. "Oh. Which reminds me."

She went in the house, and while she was inside, William ceased his work and stared at the open door. Through it he could see only the most generic details of his home—the foot of the worn-out wood stairs, leash of an old, dead dog still hanging on a hook by the coats. He felt young as a kid off to camp and at the same time old as a man leaving his wife. It was sad to think of his mother here alone, though really the situation wasn't tragic, or even new. He would come home for holidays just like he had in college. But he knew his mother perceived tragedy. And she didn't understand that it was possible to change one's perception, because she hadn't studied philosophy.

"Here," she said, reappearing in the doorway. "Some of these are due in November."

She had requested a ridiculous number of brochures. Among them were two bottom-tier schools in Chicago, which hurt William's pride. Also among them were Harvard and University of Michigan, which made him laugh. His mother said you never know. She meant this in both directions. So the whole thing was a test—she wanted to know whether he was above average or below. Earlier in the summer, they had fought about this.

Carol came around to the car's passenger side, opened the door, and placed the pile of brochures on the seat.

"Shouldn't they wear a seat belt?" he asked.

"It's up to you," she said. "I've said from the beginning, this is entirely up to you."

A silver SUV had turned down their street and was lumbering over the speed bumps.

"There they are," she said. She looked away from William, smiled hugely, and waved at the SUV. As he approached, the driver lowered his window. He was bald, faintly sunburned, wearing a bicycling shirt. He pushed back his sunglasses.

"Hayden wants to know if we can toot the horn," he said. "I told him we'd ask you."

"Sure!" Carol called.

"Not now," said the child, whom William could not see. "It's too late."

"Oh, I'm sorry," the man said. "It's too late."

"I wanted," the boy began, but didn't finish.

There was something mildly sexual about her stride as she approached the SUV. She would have denied it and acted offended if William ever pointed this out, but he was pretty sure she knew. Either way, he understood. It was part of the work. He had worked in her office the previous summer and had flirted, on instinct, with most of the women they dealt with. Even ones older than Carol.

"Can you say hi?" the man said to his kid.

"Hi, Hayden," Carol said. "Where's your mommy?"

"Mommy's feeling tired," the man said.

"Well, this is my baby," she said, opening her arm toward William. "I'm his mommy."

William came over and shook hands with the man through the open window. He ducked his head and waved at the kid, who stared at him for a second and then turned away, as if he'd seen too much.

The good-bye was stagy. Carol said the things she would have said regardless—drive safely, call from the road, you should be fine for money. She said she loved him, hugged him, let her brow crinkle up in sudden pain.

"Safe, OK?" she said. "That's all I ask."

"Mom," he said.

"I know, I know."

But it felt like an act with the client sitting there, with Hayden behind the tinted window, watching.

In Yellowstone, he got a bartending job at one of the lodges. But he'd arrived late in the season and was given the worst shifts, so he didn't send back any of his mother's money. His friend Dan was extremely cheap, and William tried to live like him. Nights William was off, which were most nights, they'd drive twenty or thirty miles out to drink in the townie bars.

Dan liked to pick up women in these places. The first time William saw this happen he thought Dan was joking. The woman's hair was teased and sprayed, and she had pink stripes of makeup on her cheeks. William remembered a drunk, sickened moment of sympathy for the woman, when he thought Dan was making a fool of her. He watched Dan smoke the woman's menthol cigarettes and pluck at one of her spaghetti straps. He remembered wanting to say, "She is a human being."

Then Dan went back to the woman's house and slept with her. Too drunk to drive, William slept in his car in the bar lot. Dan didn't have a cell phone, so in the morning William drove home and waited for him in their rented house. Even after he ate and brushed his teeth, he could still taste Jack and Coke. And in a similar way, he kept seeing the woman Dan had picked up, her bony sternum, her small, bobbing, walleyed breasts.

When the phone finally rang, he was in the middle of jerking off. He thought about ignoring it, but no, he should talk to Dan before another day and night passed. He followed the sound of the ringer till he found the cordless phone, wedged between the cushions of the couch.

"Did I wake you?"

His mother's voice confused him.

"You didn't pick up your cell," she said. "Did you lose it again?"

"Why?" he asked. "Because one time I didn't pick up?"

"Did you lend it to Dan?"

He walked to the kitchen, poured himself some water, studied the stains on the side of the filter pitcher. He gulped and let out a loud breath.

"Long night?" she asked.

"Not really," he said. "Did you call for a reason?"

She'd called to tell him he was scheduled for the October LSAT. The prep course, if he wanted to do it, began the last week of August. She thought he should, but it was up to him.

"I don't think I can take that much time off work," he said.

"Well, talk to them and let me know."

He knew she was only pretending to take him seriously, though she probably liked the idea of him having obligations. She had trouble respecting people who didn't have a schedule to consider.

"It's almost August already," he said.

"Don't I know it," she said. "The older you get, the faster time passes."

"So I guess I can't take the class," he said.

"Talk to your boss. Do you want me to talk to him?"

"No. I'll study here."

"William."

"What?"

"We had a deal," she said.

"You're right," he said. "Which part are you unhappy about? I want us both to hang up happy."

Far away in Chicago, his mother started laughing. He could see her face now, submitting to all its creases. He had told woman after woman that they were prettier when they laughed.

"Oh," she said. "I cannot wait until you have kids."

Dan did not return that evening, so William took his paperback copy of *Light in August* down to the lodge where he worked. He'd meant to read more this summer, to get through the classics he'd missed in undergrad. The bar wasn't busy, and the bartender on shift seemed to recognize him, though he didn't say hello. William ordered a beer using a shortened, familiar form of the brand name, which felt in his mouth like a code, a password that allowed him to be there.

Was it pretentious to read a book in a bar? His eyes kept shifting to the bartender. He was an older guy, twenty-seven or -eight, and he had some kind of nickname—Hecky, Henny, William couldn't remember. There was something hard and contemptuous in the way he stood, feet apart, white bar towel wound around one hand, eyes trained on the tennis match on TV as if it were trying to swindle him. William put his book away, watched tennis, tried not to look at the man again.

When he closed his tab, William saw that his two beers had been rung at full price. *I work here*, he imagined himself saying, or *hey, I—by the way, I—* But did it matter? He had money.

Where the fuck was Dan? He drove badly on his way home, not drunk but with weakened instincts. The setting sun lustered the yellow-green foothills—but was this all, finally, a cheap fairy tale? The West? Nature and beauty, wildness?

A filthy truck tapped its horn at him as he changed lanes. Yes, he gestured, it was his fault. He'd nearly missed his exit.

When he returned to Chicago, he'd missed the first session of his LSAT prep class. But it was no problem, the teacher said. He could take the first diagnostic at home. He did better than he expected—quite a bit better, in fact, and though his mother tried not to overreact, he knew she was impressed.

"Who am I to say," she said at dinner. "It seems like a waste of potential, but I don't know Dan. Maybe what he's doing is right for him."

Dan had gotten engaged. The woman was thirty-three, managed a diner, had two kids.

"He's having an experience," she said. "Every experience shapes a person."

It was raining. Leaves clogged the grates and water pooled against the curb. William looked out the restaurant window, through the white reflection of the tablecloth. The LSAT teacher said an argument was like a table. The conclusion was the top, the premises were the legs. The screws that held the top and legs together were called assumptions.

"You can't be a complete relativist," he said. "I think it's fair to say you shouldn't marry someone you've only known for six weeks."

"You're right," she said.

"There are all kinds of decisions you can make. Some are better than others."

"But you shouldn't be closed-minded."

It was not until after he took the LSAT, the real test, that he fully understood she was seeing a married man. Her client, the father of the little boy named Hayden. William was amazed at how easily he'd avoided the knowledge, and how, beginning with the moment he had put down his pencil, the truth became obvious. The proctor collected the Scantron forms, and William acknowledged that Carol was dating someone. He collected his coat and bag from the locker outside the testing room and recognized that she'd been unusually cagey about the relationship. Behind the wheel of his new car—she'd given him her 3 Series Beemer when she bought herself the 5—he recalled another dinner conversation, during which she had said how much she liked children, and how she missed William being young. At the time, he had thought this was just nostalgia. Or manipulation, a way of addressing his wish to apply to schools in California.

She might even like to do it again, she had said. She wasn't too old.

"You're forty-five," he'd said.

"Yes," she'd said, "thank you for reminding me."

She had gotten him an apartment immediately. Right on Logan Boulevard, parking included. But after the LSAT he drove to her house to see if the silver SUV was in the driveway.

It wasn't. Carol wasn't home, either.

It was only one in the afternoon, but the day had been dark with storms, and inside the house was humid and dim. William turned on the kitchen light. From the drawer under the telephone, he took a pad of her stationery. Her name was printed across the top in thick capital letters.

Hey Mom, he wrote. *Just finished the test.*

He put down the pen, went to the refrigerator, and helped himself to a beer. Six green bottles lined the shelf inside the door, one of her brands. Not her only brand, but not definitively someone else's. There was a magnet bottle opener stuck to the outside of the fridge, between photos of William at different ages and photos of her as a young mother. He used the bottle opener and replaced it with superstitious care at the angle he'd found it. Then he sat back down at the kitchen table. *Wondered if,* he wrote, but stopped. The page tore off easily.

Her ashtray on the windowsill gave off the faintest smell of resin. She'd closed the window against the rain, forcing the edge of the ashtray slightly inward, off the sill.

This is where she would have been, if she'd been home, if he'd caught her at the end of her workday, impenetrable in her tiredness. At the sound of the front door opening, she would have flicked the roach she was smoking—a portion William had always thought too petite to affect her much. She would have laid her lighter next to the ashtray. There it was now, opaque red plastic, the type she purchased in four-packs at the gas station. For gift-giving occasions over the years he had considered a better lighter. Something silver, engraved. But if she'd wanted something like that, she'd have bought it for herself.

Dear Mom, he wrote. *I just finished the test. I think it went well. I'm having a beer to celebrate. Where are you?*

He tore off this page also. He could have texted her. But he didn't want her to respond, not right this second. A note was fine.

There was thunder outside, long and muted. He felt himself at a crossroads—crossroads in a good way, in a way that he should savor. The test had gone well. It had been easier than any of the practice tests. Soon he would be in law school. He would go to California, and from there would be pulled into an adult life in which he would eventually do whatever he wanted, just as his mother now did whatever she wanted. What did it matter that she was sleeping with Hayden's father? What did it matter that Dan got married, or Katie?

Hey Mom, he wrote. *Stopped by but missed you. Hope you are well. W.*

Missed you, as in did not cross your path. Not missed you, as in longed to see you. That was clear from the context, wasn't it?

He tore off the page, folded it up with the other two drafts, and put them in his jeans pocket. Wind thumped the window but no rain fell. He finished his beer a little too fast, put the bottle in the recycling, and, pledging that this note would be the last, that no matter what it said he would leave it and leave the house, he wrote, *Mom, I'm feeling lucky. Call me later. W.*

Carol had just left a late breakfast. He'd dropped her at her office, driving his other car, sans child seat. Her parting words had been, "You do whatever you need to do," her parting gesture to kiss him quickly on the cheek, like a friend. Then she hurried from the curb to her office door, ducking slightly against the threat of rain.

"Fuck you," she said softly, chuckling as she unlocked the door.

Oh, things were so much better now, in this phase of her life. She could read the leaves now, she had become almost psychic. She'd read somewhere that being psychic was nothing supernatural. It was just an extreme form of getting it. She got it now. She actually got it.

"Focus," she said aloud. No one was in the office today, a Saturday. She turned on the overhead lights, which were warm and flattered the room. Up front the receptionist's desk was chic and immaculate, and Carol's own desk, which was much less organized, was concealed by a Japanese screen. William's workstation was just a laptop at an oblong, Danish-design table—the exact right tone for the room, fashionable, casual, productive.

Near his laptop was a white paper coffee cup, left behind the last time he came in. Even that seemed somehow perfect.

She carried the cup to the kitchenette, opened the cupboard under the sink, and as a reflex took a last sip before throwing it away. Right away she recognized her mistake, but not soon enough to stop from swallowing. She winced and held the cup away from her face, eyeing the pale brown stain that crept along its seam. It actually hadn't tasted so awful. She would have to tease him about how much sugar he used.

Six weeks later, the results of William's test came back.

"This is my son," Carol said to the hostess at the restaurant. She put her arm around his back and pressed her cheek against the shoulder of his wool coat. "He doesn't want me to tell you this, but." She looked at him, and he grinned at her, and she pursed her own smile, as if to keep it from flying off her face.

"He's a very, very intelligent young man," she said. "That's all."

"Two for dinner," William said.

"We're celebrating," Carol added.

"Congratulations," the hostess said, and looked genuine about it. How could she not be genuinely happy for them? A mother and son who were good friends, in love, mother-son love, sharing a triumph. How could that not beam out to everyone and make them want a part of it?

"She's cute," Carol said when they were seated. "You should ask for her number."

"Maybe I will," William said. He and Carol had had the same cocktail before dinner.

"Do you want me to do it for you?"

"Do you really think that's the best approach?"

Carol chuckled. "What on earth could you mean?"

They went through two bottles of wine. Hundred-dollar bottles, and everything they wanted to eat, dessert, free limoncello from the owner. The night was charmed so that neither of them could get too drunk, no matter how much they had. But William took the keys from the valet and helped her into the passenger seat of her car. It was December now, a fragile snow falling and melting instantly on the roads. Christmas lights downtown, streets full of theatergoers.

"Let's go somewhere else," she said. "The Tavern on Rush."

"Why, so we can score some coke?"

"No!"

"So we can marry you off to a day trader?"

"You don't do cocaine, do you, William?"

"I don't. Do you?"

"Good lord, no," she said. "Not in ages."

"I don't know how I feel about Rush Street," he said.

"I know where," she said, and reached for the steering wheel.

"Easy, easy," he said. "Just tell me."

"Press that button," she said. "On the side of the wheel."

He did. The Bluetooth lit up and the computer's voice said, "Name, please."

"The Peninsula Hotel," Carol shouted.

It was one o'clock in the morning when they got back to her house. They went through the back door, and William stood in the kitchen watching as she got her cigarettes out of the honey-bear cookie jar on top of the fridge. "I swear I hardly ever smoke," she said, handing him one. On the back porch, under the lip of the roof, she bent over the flame of her lighter, and William reached forward to shield the wind. He saw her face in profile, in the glow of that little flame, high cheekbones and slightly upturned nose, faint scowl as she concentrated on her cigarette. The pleasure of seeing her, her beauty and familiarity, crested and dissolved into something almost sickening. But then the light went out, and they stood in the sparkling cold, mother and son again, and she said, "I am so fucking proud of you."

"I swear, sometimes I think about Jesus," she went on. "And I get it. It's like, it took forty thousand years for me to put it together, that it's not about faith and saving the poor and all that condescending hypocritical *shit*."

He listened. He smoked. This was hilarious.

"It's about the baby," she went on. "It's like—Christmas Day. The child is born."

She paused for a long time.

"You die for your baby. You die for the rest of your life so your baby can live, and your baby lives so you can die."

"Whoa, Mom," he said.

"What am I talking about?" she said, and she looked at him and gave a slack smile. "I should go to bed."

The only word she said after that was, "Night." They went in. She unzipped her boots with surprising grace and went upstairs. But alone in the dark downstairs the star-white alcohol halo stayed around his body. He wheeled into the kitchen, for water, for dark and a window with winter behind it. It had not always been so safe in this house. Tonight was the future.

Then, an hour. Water, television, and things flattened again. She was upstairs on top of the duvet in her dress. He drove himself back to his place.

His test score was not enough to get him into the schools in California. He spent eight excruciating weeks on the wait-list at the last of them, before being encouraged to reapply next year.

The deal was not that he would reapply next year.

He enrolled at a school in Chicago. Carol didn't know why he was so negative about it. It was a perfectly good school, and this way he didn't have the hassle of packing and moving.

Just before school started, he stood up in Dan's wedding, and after the party he slept with one of the bridesmaids. She was ten years older than he was. She was a little rough with him, so he was a little rough with her. In the morning he apologized, and she said, "Sorry for what?"

Then it was December again.

He asked Carol not to call him during the week before final exams, and she obeyed with theatrical seriousness. She rarely saw him these days, she told her friends, he was just so busy. Halfway through the week, she left him a voicemail, shaming herself for calling, then asking what he wanted for Christmas.

In the beginning he was earnest about studying. He covered his desk and coffee table with books spread open, decorated them liberally with pencil and highlighter. The work was not uninteresting and he was not incapable. He took breaks only to shower, to eat, and at night he had textureless dreams about the Socratic method. He had impulses to call her but refrained.

The morning of his first exam he woke to his cell phone alarm. Head still down, he silenced the noise. Nine more minutes he slept, phone under his pillow, till the alarm went off again.

This time he powered the phone down and let it slip into the crack between the bed and wall.

He stayed in bed for several hours, studying the snow as it thickened on the ledge outside his window. Somewhere an analog clock snipped away the minutes of a test on civil procedure. His phone remained where he'd dropped it, somewhere under the bed. He could go a few days without answering. But eventually she would worry. He would have to explain.

I'm feeling lucky, he imagined saying, and laughed internally, and then aloud. *Hey, Mom—*

NELL

She was nine years older than Christopher. Right away, she was candid about her age. She sat on the bar's rooftop patio all through a perfect Seattle summer, drinking wine with her friends, and after her friends left in taxis she came inside and had one more, sometimes two. The name on her credit card receipt was Ellen M. Borgman, but she introduced herself as Nell.

"I'm not old enough to be your mother," she told him. "But I could've been your babysitter."

Christopher ducked to look for a bottle on the shelf under the bar. Then he took down a port glass and poured her a taste of something they'd just gotten in.

"Didn't you ever have a crush on your babysitter?" she asked.

"Of course." He took down another glass and poured himself the same, drank quickly, and ducked again to put the glass in the bus tub. He turned to the computer, printed the check for one of his tables. He tried to keep moving when he was at work.

The rooftop patio closed for the fall, when the rain began again, so now Nell and her friends sat indoors. One of the friends was several months pregnant and drank soda water with a few drops of bitters. Christopher didn't charge her. He asked if she was having the baby at Swedish.

"My daughter was born there," he said.

"What'd you think?" the woman asked.

He glanced at Nell, and Nell noticed.

"They were great," he said. "We loved the nurses."

"I've heard great things," the woman said. She wasn't as attractive as Nell but she was attractive. She had lines in her forehead, but her lips were full, her teeth pretty, her hair thick, shiny, and natural. Briefly, he imagined a life with a woman like her.

"How old is your daughter?" Nell asked. Her voice changed when she drank too much, became high-pitched like a teenage girl flirting. Not always, but sometimes. In a certain way, he liked it.

"Four in February," he said.

"What's her name?" another woman asked. This woman was attractive also. All Nell's friends were, and they all liked him.

"Molly."

"Oh my God, that's adorable."

Nell was gazing at him, sweetly and shamelessly, and again he sensed the teenage girl inside the grown woman.

"Do you have a picture?"

"My phone's behind the bar."

He checked on his other tables, talked with the DJ, who had his turntables set up by the entrance. Christopher bought him a cocktail and told him they'd find him a better spot. The DJ was cool, but kind of shy, and talking to him could get boring.

When Christopher brought the women their check, he also brought his phone.

"I got this," Nell said, taking the check. Christopher pulled up a photo of Molly in Buzz Lightyear pajamas and handed the phone to the pregnant woman.

"She's amazing," the woman said. "Oh my God, look at this."

Buzz Lightyear is her hero, he wanted to tell them. She hates princesses. She won't wear bows. But he didn't want to seem political. Most of these women wore wedding rings, probably had kids, and he didn't care what their kids liked.

Nell put her AmEx in the pocket of the check cover. "I said no," she said when her friends tried to give her money. "I'm having a good year."

"You don't wear a ring," she said to Christopher when her friends had gone home. "Is that a bartender thing? Tips or whatever?"

"I'm not married," he said.

"That makes me happy."

He looked at the labels on the bottles under the bar. She liked earthy wines, which were trendy, which women liked because women were supposed to like other things. Or, he didn't know, maybe she just liked the taste.

"You're not driving, are you?" he asked.

"I'll leave my car here."

"Will you? Or will you say that and then plow it into a lamppost?"

"Plow it," she said. "What are you pouring?"

"I'll call a taxi."

"But not yet. Please, not yet?"

He poured them each a half glass and gave her water also.

"Does your daughter live with you?"

"Yeah," he said. "There's no way she wouldn't. Her mom lives with us too."

"Oh."

"Her mom's not very—" He shouldn't be doing this. Complaining to a woman who clearly wanted him. "It's better for my daughter if we all live together," he said.

"So, are you—"

"Yes. We are."

"That makes me sad." Nell was flushed and her eyes were very blue. "But I get it."

"Hang on," he said. "I'll be back."

There was one more table to close out, and there was the DJ to pay. He'd already sent home the prep cook, who dealt with the cheese plates and olives, and now he tipped out Gabe, the barback, who glanced at Nell, then gave Christopher a questioning look. "She's almost done," Christopher said. Whatever else Gabe was trying to ask, he didn't need to take up with him. Gabe was weird about women.

"Drink that," he said to Nell, pointing at her water when everyone was gone.

She gulped till the glass was empty. He could see not just the teenager but a much younger child in her now. Alcohol did this to some people, but not to everyone. Not to Nell until tonight. It was disturbing, this power he had because he had a daughter. He thought of Molly growing up to be—but no. He left Molly out of it.

"I'm sorry," she said, putting the glass down.

"For what?"

"Being a drunken old hag, hanging around here all the time."

Under the bar they kept dishes of nuts covered in plastic and dated with black marker. He put one on the bar and took off the plastic.

"Being a middle-aged lush," she said. "Getting old and dying."

"Stop that," he said.

He knew she wanted him to say she was beautiful. His girl-friend did all kinds of things to get him to say it.

"I know," she said. "There's nothing less attractive than self-pity."

He could think of a few things. Slapping your kid, for example. What was she supposed to do, his girlfriend had asked. Another fucking time-out? Molly'd been in time-out all fucking day. "Tell me!" his girlfriend had screamed. "Because I don't know."

Gabe came out from the kitchen, coat zipped, backpack on his shoulder. He said hello to Nell, then looked at Christopher.

"Taking off soon?" Gabe asked.

"Right after you. We're just waiting for her cab."

"I shouldn't be driving," Nell said, as if this were a joke.

Gabe looked at Christopher again. For fuck's sake. Christopher looked back at him neutrally.

"See you Saturday," Gabe said finally.

Christopher followed him to the door, and when he was gone, he locked the door behind him. Then he lowered the shade behind the glass. He heard Nell step off her barstool, heard her shoes on the floor, and pretended she'd gotten up to go to the ladies' room, until he felt her hand on his shoulder. Then she was kissing him.

"Hey," he said after a minute. "Hey, hey, hey."

"I'm sorry."

Hey, hey, hey was exactly what his father used to say when one of Christopher's sisters was crying. Or Christopher himself.

"I'll call you a taxi."

"Don't."

She was kissing him and she smelled wonderful, and for a minute he put his arms around her and felt his body becoming insistent.

"OK," he said, pushing her gently away, holding her shoulders.

"Please," she said. There was a kink of hurt between her eyebrows, as if she were remembering something privately painful, something Christopher didn't want to know.

"I can't," he said.

She opened her eyes, then closed them. He waited what felt like a long time for her to say something.

"Will you tell me about your daughter? I want to know her name."

He brought Nell back to the bar, refilled her water, and from the cordless phone by the computer he called a cab company. While he waited for an operator he poured himself more wine, and when she asked, he poured her as little as he could without seeming condescending. Nell gazed out at the empty tables, smiling a little.

"I can't believe I did that. I'm sorry."

He put the phone on speaker and set it on the bar. The hold music was "Taxman" by the Beatles, which sounded ugly and aggressive.

"Nothing to be sorry about," he said.

He closed out the register, collected the long tongue of paper from the printer, circled the total with a green highlighter pen. He counted out his tips in cash. Normally, he did this in the office, normally thought very dimly of what he'd do if he were robbed. Of what he could use as a weapon—the owner had a trophy on the desk, a wine award won a long time ago, before the owner was old and divorced. He thought of how he'd feel if he ended up killing the intruder. Terrible. Terrified. He knew this, but couldn't really imagine it.

"We appreciate your patience," the taxi service said.

"Molly," Nell said. "You already told me her name."

He'd made two twenty, not great, and fifty of that was Nell's much too large tip. She didn't have to do that, but he didn't want to have an awkward conversation about it. Out of habit, he turned his back when he put the cash in his wallet. Then he leaned his elbows on the bar, moved the dish of nuts so it was between them, ate a few.

"She probably loves you so much," Nell said.

He pushed back off his elbows and grabbed a cocktail napkin to put under her water glass. "She does," he said. "I love her so much."

"Little kids just love so hard—we can't even remember how that feels." Nell picked up her wineglass with both hands, sipped, and then stared into it. "I remember my dad carrying me when I fell asleep in the car. I would fake that I was still asleep because I never wanted him to put me down."

The taxi service's hold music switched to Janis Joplin, to the words *down on me* exactly at the moment Nell said *put me down.* Christopher wanted to point out the coincidence but knew it was the wrong thing to say. "Whenever I'm being serious," his girlfriend had accused him, "nothing comes out of your mouth that isn't a fucking joke." *Fuck you,* he thought, *would you prefer that?* But he always stopped himself. Adult life was vigilance against sinking to a certain level. Not for everyone. Not for his girlfriend. Jesus Christ, not for her. When he first met her she'd been different. Or no, she was always this way, but he'd thought it was only a posture, the way she didn't give a fuck. He'd thought—he didn't remember what he'd thought.

"Yellow Cab sucks," he said, picking up the cordless. "I'm calling City."

The number for City Cab was under the number for Yellow, on a scrap of paper taped to the side of the computer. When he turned back to Nell, she was gazing at him again. She was really pretty.

The operator picked up right away.

"Fifteen to twenty minutes," he said when he hung up, and then he leaned across the bar and put his hand on the side of Nell's face and kissed her. He pulled away for a second to push the glasses and dish of nuts down the bar, then reached for her. She was standing up, then climbing on the barstool, and as he kissed her again he pulled her over the bar and held her as she felt for the floor with her feet.

"I can't," he said.

"I know," she said, unbuttoning his jeans.

He felt bad when she was on her knees on the black rubber mat, about her nice gray pants getting dirty and about his hand on her head, trying not to pull her closer, trying only to touch her in some way, to tell her he thought she was beautiful, he wasn't just—

She pushed his hand away and he leaned back into the liquor shelf. He thought of Gabe coming back, having forgotten something. Of his girlfriend calling. And he thought, fuck it. It felt good. She wasn't in love with him. She was just some fucked-up woman, and he was just some fucked-up guy.

When it was over, she sat back on her heels and looked up at him. He'd known she was drunk, but the way she looked now, her hand still holding her hair in a fist by her jaw, her sad, happy, drunk face leaning heavily on her fist, made him feel like a criminal. He went to put new ice in her water glass.

"Here," he said, turning around.

He missed what happened next. Trying to stand, she'd lurched into the ledge under the liquor shelves, not falling completely but ending up clutching her face. One high-heeled shoe had caught in the mesh of the rubber mat and now stood upright a few steps behind her. He cringed at the thought of her bare foot on the filthy mat, and stupidly picked up the shoe.

"Fuck me," she moaned, cradling her face.

"Are you OK?"

When she took her hands away, her mouth and chin were covered in blood.

"I don't know," she said. Then she saw the blood on her hands and started crying.

"It's OK. It's going to be fine."

Clean dishcloth, cold water. Nell sat on a barstool crying while he wiped away the blood. There was a small horizontal gash under her bottom lip, not wide but deep. A fair amount of blood on the cloth.

"You might—" he began, and felt dread seep into his body, lies to tell his girlfriend coming to him as if he were shouting them into his own ears. One thing at a time. "You should probably go to the hospital," he said. Not wanting to, he continued, "I can take you."

She blinked, little feathers of mascara clinging to the wet skin under her eyes. Then she closed her eyes and leaned toward him, mouth open. He took a step back.

"Hold that," he said, moving her hand to the cloth on her chin.

Six-top fifteen minutes before close, he texted his girlfriend. *Should I just kick them out?*

He gave Nell her shoe. "Is it still bleeding?"

She moved the cloth away from her face. Bright blood filled the cut and slipped down her chin, which he'd just wiped clean.

"Keep pressure on it," he said.

She was crying again. "You won't even kiss me."

He moved her hand back to her chin and held the cloth against the cut. On the counter behind the bar, his phone vibrated. He put his arm around Nell in a half hug, rubbing her back a little. He couldn't see his phone, but it was obvious who had texted. He imagined what she might've written: *What's the six-top's name? What does the six-top look like?* Or maybe, *You're a liar.* If so, good. He was so fucking sick of—OK. One thing at a time. The bar phone was ringing. The automated voice told him the cab would arrive in approximately six minutes.

He went around the bar, put the phone on its charger. Then he checked his texts. *Kick em out*, she'd written. *Come home and kiss me.*

"That's the cab," he said.

Nell sat very still on the barstool, holding her shoe in her lap, staring off again with a small, vacant smile.

The emergency room was a nightmare; it could be hours.

"I think I can drive," she said.

"You need to go to the hospital." *Probably an hour*, he texted. "I said I'd take you."

Before he went back to the office to grab his coat and bag, he poured a sip of bourbon, drank it, and put the glass in the bus tub. Nell was still sitting with her eyes closed, maybe near passing out or maybe just being emotional. She'd have to sober up before they'd give her stitches. He remembered that from college.

They went out the back. When the motion sensor lights lit the alley, he felt another wave of dread, more acute this time. He kept a little distance from her, but worried she'd fall in those shoes or drop the fresh cloth she held to her face. He had the other two bloody cloths balled in his hand, and after he locked up, he crossed the alley and tossed them in one of the residential garbage cans. Stupid thoughts came—SVU detectives, DNA—so stupid he almost laughed. He scanned the windows in the buildings across the alley, found two still lit but no one looking out. The outline of a computer monitor in one, square halo of white. People had their own lives.

"Tell me about your daughter," she said, turning suddenly. She was a few steps ahead, walking with a lurching confidence that seemed to come from the shoes. At this distance, she was the woman she'd been when she first walked into the bar. Slender, successful. He didn't want to tell her, or any woman ever again, about his daughter.

She waited for him to walk beside her. He walked a little ahead, leading her toward the car, his mother's old station wagon, which she'd given him when Molly was born. As he opened the passenger door for Nell, it occurred to him to be embarrassed. Then, seeing the child seat in back, he felt how stupid the whole situation was and said nothing. He closed the door carefully, making sure she was all the way in.

"She must be so beautiful," Nell said as they drove.

He was taking her to Swedish, the first hospital that came to mind. He should ask where she lived.

"Don't let go of that," he said. "Keep pressure on it."

At the hospital, there'd be people who could do something for her. He felt for his phone but didn't check it. He'd said an hour. And even if she found out, OK.

"You're nice," Nell said.

The streets were mostly empty. Cars on the road but almost no one on the sidewalks. Taxis, the closer they got to downtown, as he drove east past expensive hotels. In the entrance of one, a young man was tipping the valet who'd brought around his black Mercedes. Or maybe not his. That guy could be someone's assistant. Who knew who had what?

"I'll drop you at the emergency room," Christopher said. "But after that I've got to go. I wish I didn't."

Without looking at him, she put her hand on his arm.

"Sorry, I—" He moved his elbow. "I have to steer."

"I know," she said.

He was driving past hospital buildings now. He tried to follow the signs. There was the birth center. Molly had been born in the daytime; he'd never really looked at the place in the dark. The day after she was born, when Christopher's father came to the hospital to visit, his mother went out to the lobby, saying she needed to make a phone call. Holding Molly, his father had cried.

"This is my fault," Nell said. "I know that."

Emergency was south, the signs said. And it was, in a way, her fault. He didn't have to say it wasn't.

"Will you be OK?" he asked when he'd pulled up to the emergency room entrance.

"I'm a fucking idiot," she said to the windshield.

He should tell her to call him, to let him know everything was all right. But he didn't want to give her his phone number.

"Make sure they get you a cab home."

She looked at him. The spot on the cloth was small, the bleeding less.

"I guess good-bye," she said.

She waited a minute before she unbuckled her seat belt and reached to open the door. Maybe he should've gotten up to help her, but she seemed fine.

"I'm sure I'll see you," he said when she was almost out of the car.

She ducked to look at him again. He wanted her to shut the door and go. When she finally did, the sound hurt him a little, the sudden loudness of the heater and the engine, because he knew he—but he hadn't—but she was anyway. Hurt. And he was relieved. He waited for the glass doors to open for her, watched her stop and take out her phone. See, she had people. She was fine.

He turned on the radio, a little loud, catching the end of a song he'd liked in high school. Eleven years now since he'd finished high school and Molly was eleven years from starting. That'd never happen again, that symmetry.

It was a stupid song, from that period of corny pop punk. He couldn't remember the name of the band. But it reminded him of hot-boxing the station wagon, the one he was still driving now.

It reminded him of a girl who wouldn't be his girlfriend even though she snuck him into her dad's apartment many nights after parties. There'd been girls who would've been his girlfriend, but he never wanted them. Siobhan Gallagher was her name, and he remembered waiting in the little enclosed courtyard while she found her keys, remembered a lone potted cactus on the window ledge. Her dad had traveled a lot.

He had time, so he drove back to the bar instead of home. *They've got their check*, he texted. No blood on the shelf or floor where she'd fallen. No lipstick, even, on the water glass still left on the bar, not that it would've mattered. She wasn't wearing any, or it had worn off.

He sprayed the shelf and bar and wiped them down, waiting while his imaginary six-top found their coats, made their loud, marginally funny parting jokes. Maybe one thanked him, or made some odd, unwanted promise.

He would slip in and kiss Molly when he got home. He could do it without waking her. But for now, for just a minute, it felt so good to be alone.

DIRETORA

avi and I were taking acting. We'd learned how to fake a slap. One night in the dorm, we practiced.

"Just leave me alone," I said, with what I hoped was passion.

"Don't walk away from me," he said.

"I said leave me alone."

He came close, raised his hand, and swiped it across the air in front of my face. I jerked my head to the side and at the same time clapped my hands sharply, down by my hip.

"That was good," Andrew said. He was watching from his bed, propped up with his Greek homework on his lap.

"You turned too soon," Davi said. "Don't look at my hand, look me in the eye." He put his hands on my shoulders. "I'll do it slow," he said.

He raised his hand and in slow motion drew the arc of the slap. When his hand was just barely in front of my face, I turned my head, also in slow motion.

"Smack," Davi said. "You're still not looking me in the eye."

"Yes, I am," I said.

"Woman," he said. "I know when someone's looking me in the eye."

"Man," I said. "I am looking you in the eye. These are eyes, right?" I pointed at mine. "What's the word in Portuguese?"

"That's it, you little—" He swiped his hand in front of my face again, and I jerked my head to the side but forgot to clap.

"That was better," Andrew said. "That looked really real."

"*Olho, puta*," Davi said, laughing. "How do you say 'eyes'? That was good."

"Do it again," I said.

Andrew was my boyfriend and Davi was his roommate. My room was right next door, but I was always in theirs. Davi didn't care if I slept over. He'd almost walked in once when I was straddling Andrew, totally naked, but by the time he got the door unlocked Andrew had pulled me down and thrown the blanket over us. "Oh my God," Davi had said, "I'm hiding my eyes." He covered his eyes with his hand and went to his closet, a particle-board cupboard at the foot of his twin bed, exactly like Andrew's. "Dude, I'm sorry," Andrew said. "I thought you were—" "I am," Davi said, and with his hand still over his eyes held up a three-strip of condoms, and Andrew and I laughed. "Bye, Mom and Dad," he said as he went out the door again. "Don't wait up."

At night, the three of us lay in the dark talking about what people looked like. We went up and down the halls of the dorm: Amber was OK. You could fuck her, why not? Lindsey was too tall, she wasn't ugly but was kind of like a dude. Marcus was attractive, I said. Not as attractive as Andrew. Or Davi. Right, they said. But it was true! Davi made a rule: no one in the dorm was as attractive as we were. Who else? Richard we shouldn't talk about, he was only fourteen, the youngest person ever enrolled at the university. But why shouldn't we talk about him?

When Davi and Andrew were fourteen, they were both already having sex.

I'd never had a boyfriend before Andrew. I'd had sex, but just a few times, in parents' bedrooms or little kids' bedrooms at parties. This email quiz had gone around the dorm, the Purity Test, and my score was the same as Andrew's because I'd done more drugs. Davi was the least pure. He was the only one who'd been with two people at once.

"Just leave me alone," I said now.

"Don't walk away from me."

"I said leave me alone."

I looked him in the eye. He was right that I hadn't before, though I thought I had. Really looking him in the eye felt different.

"You're still looking at my hand," he said. "At the last second, you look at my hand."

"Because you're laughing," I said. "I can see it in your eyes. You're not really angry. It's just a game for you."

"Is this what acting is?" Andrew asked.

"Pretty much," Davi said.

"Flaky," Andrew said.

"Pretty much," Davi and I said, almost in unison, and then laughed.

"Can you go do this somewhere else?" Andrew asked. "I've got shit to do."

"Listen, you fucking Greek," Davi said. "Don't get aggressive with me. Your civilization crumbled, remember?"

"I remember. So pillage my woman. Get her out of here so I can learn these verbs."

They both looked at me, waiting for me to object. I opened the door and stepped halfway out into the hall.

"Just leave me alone," I said.

One weekend when Davi was away skiing with kids from his prep school, Andrew and I had watched a bunch of porn. He couldn't believe I'd never seen one. "Catholic girls," he said, "it's so fucking true." It was true. I'd hardly even kissed anyone without being really drunk. The first time he got me off, I started crying. No one had ever done that to me when I was sober.

"Don't walk away from me," Davi said, following me into the hall.

"I said leave me alone."

"That's shitty dialogue," Andrew called.

"I'm beating my wife," Davi said. "It can't be Shakespeare."

"Hamlet fucked with Ophelia pretty bad."

"He was a prince. I'm just Kowalski. People from Poland are Poles, bitch."

Davi pulled the door shut. There was no one else in the hall. He put his hands on my shoulders again, then pointed at his eyes.

"But you can't be laughing," I said. "You have to be pissed. What did I do to you?"

"You fucked someone else," he said, shaking me a little.

"But you're laughing about it. Is it funny? Do you care?"

"You're good at this," he said. "You should be a director."

Davi was free with compliments. I'd heard him tell this girl from the third floor she should be a dancer. But I still liked it when he complimented me.

"OK," he said. He let go of me and took a step back, bounced on his toes a little, pumped his arms like a boxer.

"You're furious," I said.

"Furious." He snarled at me, showing straight, white upper teeth.

"No," I said. "It's still just a game."

"It's not a game, bitch," he said, lunging toward me.

The women's bathroom door opened and Honni, this South African girl from the end of the hall, stepped out in a towel, wet blond hair combed flat. She glanced at us, then quickly went the other way.

"Ah, we're just playing," Davi called after her.

"Acting," I said. Davi's English was perfect except for the rare wrong idiom.

"I wondered," Honni said. She held her neon net bag of toiletries up by her chest, fist above heart, securing the towel. "You're good at it, yeah? I thought something was really wrong."

Andrew, Davi, and I agreed that Honni was attractive. The accent, I'd said, and Andrew said not just the accent, and over in his bed, alone, Davi laughed.

"Check this out," he said to her now. "Don't walk away from me."

"I said leave me alone," I said.

We did the slap. The timing was perfect, but my clap was off. It was supposed to be fast and sharp and should hurt a little.

"Bravo," Honni said.

Davi checked out her ass as she walked down the hall. She had pale, pretty legs and her wet hair was parted down the back of her head. He was imagining himself behind her, staring into the white line of her part, hands on her hips, or I guess I was the one imagining it. When Andrew and I watched those videos, it took only a couple of minutes before we were fucking.

We did more than just fuck, though. Andrew had cried in front of me a bunch of times. He'd gone off Prozac in September, wanting college to be different. He didn't need it—his stepfather had prescribed it, this cynical, sinewy old guy, who'd slept in a low-oxygen tent in the living room all summer, preparing to climb Everest.

When Andrew cried and I held him it was almost as good as sex. But afterward, he'd get kind of cold, and say things like the rip in the back pocket of my jeans was whorish, not even sexy, just desperate.

I knew how to say fuck you. I knew how to disappear for a day or two until he panicked. I don't know how I knew these things, but I was glad I did.

"Should we switch it?" I asked Davi when Honni was gone. "Should it be that you cheated on me?"

"With her?" he said. "No."

"What about with Jessie? Or that sorority girl from Halloween?"

"No, no, no," he said. "You cheated on me. I wouldn't hit you if I cheated on you."

"Are you sure?"

He thought about it. "Right, because of the guilt," he said.

He looked at my mouth for a second, then off to the side. Just faintly, he winced. "I'm thinking about these guys in Brazil," he said. "They're such pieces of shit. But they're my friends, you know?"

"What's it like to be one of them?" I asked.

He looked surprised, then hurt. "I'm not," he said.

"No, I mean imagine you are," I said. "For the scene."

"Oh, yeah, yeah." The hurt cleared from his face. "*Diretora.* OK. I'm a piece of shit."

"But you don't think that," I said. "You think you're in the right."

"No, that's wrong," Davi said. "I know I'm shit, that's why I'm angry. You're supposed to make me better, but instead you—"

Their door opened and Andrew leaned out. "I can hear every word you're saying even with headphones on," he said. "Go somewhere else."

He had his headphones around his neck, and I could hear the white noise coursing through them. I didn't believe he could really hear us with them on. Andrew had a hard time concentrating just in general, and it was always a big drama.

"You missed Honni," Davi said. "In a towel."

"Fuck, really?" Andrew grinned.

There was this guy on the first floor, Roark, who had been in the computer lab when Andrew took the Purity Test, and now he was always talking to Andrew about sex, in this immature way that made it really obvious he was a virgin. When I was around, Roark looked at me like he knew a secret, like he could blackmail me if he wanted. Andrew said he probably thought about me when he jerked off. "I mean, you and half the girls in this dorm," he said. "Don't be too flattered." "Yeah, I was really flattered," I said.

"You're acting like Roark," I said now.

"Me?" Andrew asked.

"Yeah."

Andrew stared at me. "You're acting like a cunt," he said.

"Oh, hurt me."

"Guys," Davi said. "This is ugly. He's got work to do, OK? Leave him alone."

Andrew slammed the door. The slam echoed foolishly in the hall. I was embarrassed for Andrew and sick of him, but I was still going to sleep in his bed tonight. My roommate was in our room listening to Christian rock, and I was too timid to ask her to turn it off even when she offered.

"Leave him alone?" I asked. "Leave me alone."

I ran down the hall, almost to the end where it opened into a little common space. A couple kids were spread out on the couches, studying.

"Don't you fucking walk away," Davi said, running after me.

"I said leave me alone."

He caught up with me, caught me by the arms. I tried to shake him off, still crying out a little, adding more words to the scene. The slap wasn't very good—I forgot to look him in the eye—but I stumbled into the common space when I recoiled and held my face like I was in pain. The kids who were studying looked up at us, and Davi grabbed my hand, lifted it up in the air, and swung us down into a bow.

"Thank you very much," he said. Then, still holding my hand, he ran across the common space and into the opposite hall.

"That was great," he said. "Let's do it again."

"Just leave me alone," I shouted, racing toward the computer lab. He caught up with me right in front of the lab and we played out the scene in the doorway. This time, I looked him right in the eye.

"Just a joke," I called out to the staring kids in the computer lab. Richard the fourteen-year-old was in there, crouching in front of a screen.

"What kind of joke is that?" I heard a girl say, but we were already gone.

We ran back through the common space, but instead of heading back toward our rooms, we veered out into the dark dining hall. The kitchen was closed and there was no one in there.

"Leave . . . me . . . the fuck . . . alone," I gasped.

"Get back here, bitch."

"I said—"

He caught up with me faster than I expected and already had his hand up to slap me. I met his eyes and felt all his anger and confusion merging with mine and as I said the rest of my line I lurched toward him so that when he swept his hand across the air it clipped my mouth and chin.

"Oh my God," he cried. "I'm so sorry. I'm so sorry."

I covered my face with my hands. It didn't hurt that much, just stung, but the adrenaline brought this antiseptic taste to my mouth and I was scared something had happened to my teeth.

"Let me see. Let me see."

I let him pull my hands off my face. I was laughing. The tears, which hadn't been much, were almost gone.

"Oh," he said, and he grabbed me and hugged me hard. "I am so sorry."

"It's fine, I'm OK," I said. We were swaying backward a little, and I took a couple of steps to keep from falling.

He pulled back and looked at my chin. "You're not bleeding. You're not bruised. Let's go in the light and see if you're going to have a bruise."

"I won't," I said.

"What the fuck happened?"

"It was my fault."

We walked back toward the common space. Only one girl was still sitting there studying, this girl Deanna, who was hot but bulimic. She pretended not to watch as Davi tipped my head back and examined my chin under the light.

"It doesn't look bad," he said. "I think it's going to be OK."

"That was good," I said, staring at the speckled, fireproof ceiling. "We were getting it."

THE CHEESECAKE FACTORY

My father apologizes for giving advice. He says he knows everyone's probably giving us advice these days and we're probably tired of it. He says we're probably suspicious of the motivations behind all this advice, including his, because people who give advice are usually just rehearsing a defense of their own choices. He says that's true, that's true a lot of the time, and though he believes in his particular case it's not entirely true, who is he kidding? Most people think they are the exception to the rule, but if most people were the exception, the rule would be something else.

He says we're probably wondering when this preface is going to end and when we'll actually get to hear the advice he's planning to give.

"The preface is a little long," I say.

Then he'll cut to the chase, he says. He doesn't think we should wait to have kids.

He knows, he knows, everyone is probably telling us this, but here's the thing. He doesn't care about grandkids. It's not grandkids he wants, he's not one of those people. Maybe it's something wrong with him or something to do with Simon still being just seven years old. Simon still needs a dad. Not that I, his daughter, don't need a dad, but it's different, isn't it? He means I don't need help tying my shoes or someone to cut up my food for me. Not that I don't need a father anymore, people always need their parents, though maybe not him, but that's because he never really had parents. He had Dickensian villains for parents, which he knows is an exaggeration but in some ways is completely true, too.

My husband, Jordan, laughs politely, which is what my father seems to want. My father glances at him, appreciating the laugh, appreciating that Jordan knows what *Dickensian* means. Dad likes Jordan, whom he's met many times, but he doesn't know him well enough to feel quite comfortable. It's hard to say if my father knows anyone that well.

Right now he's wondering—I can see this in the quick squint that comes before he smiles—how much I've told Jordan about him. Where he comes from, how he grew up. He's wondering if I've gotten it right, if I really know the story. How much has Dad even told me, and how much have I listened?

We're at the Cheesecake Factory in the Oakbrook shopping center, sharing spinach dip and drinking. Red wine for me, white wine for Dad, beer for my husband. Dad sits in what seems an uncomfortable position on his side of the booth, one shoulder back and one forward—his back must be bothering him. One of his hands is palm flat on the vinyl upholstery, the other balled in a fist on the table. He's trying not to eat too much dip. I'm pretty sure he's counting loosely in his head, spreading out the time between bites. He puts two corn chips on his bread plate, dips one and eats it, then balls up his fist again and waits sixty seconds before he eats the other. He's in town on business, just for one night, a Tuesday. Jordan and I drove out to the suburbs to meet him at his Marriott.

"How's everything tasting?" our server asks. She's a tall, heavyset woman with unnaturally solicitous mannerisms. My father doesn't like her.

"One more of these?" she asks, picking up his wineglass.

"That'd be great," he says. His voice is friendly, but he cringes from her physically, in a way so obvious I start to worry about her feelings.

When she's gone, he makes a face that means he finds her annoying. Jordan laughs.

"So I was saying," Dad says, and then, interrupting himself, asks, "Do you think I love Simon more than I love you?"

"No," I say.

"Because honestly, I don't."

"I know," I say. "Why would I think that?"

"I don't know," he says, "but I don't. But I'll tell you one thing. It is so much easier raising Simon with Eileen than it was raising you kids with your mother. So much easier when you're not in constant conflict. When you can just enjoy being parents together. And this gets back to what I was saying about you guys."

He grabs one last chip before the busboy takes the basket.

"You don't need to wait till you have enough money. Money you can figure out. Hell, if I'd waited till I had enough money, I wouldn't have had kids till I was forty-five."

"Well, you were forty-eight when you had Simon," I say. "And you had way more money than you did with Mom."

"Yeah," Dad says, and his inflection rises as if he sees my point, but for a moment he's distracted, back in an old warp of feelings about my mother. How she forced a hasty, hateful divorce. How money went flying, the house went at a devastating loss. This didn't matter to my mother, who almost immediately remarried a wealthy man and started buying art, a grand piano, property in Santa Fe. Dad is thinking of that first, bare Christmas, alone with us kids in the unsold house, from which my mother had already moved her half of the furniture. He has two or three choice lines of invective to quote, insults she added to outrageous injury, which alone justify his conclusion on the matter: He will never, never, never, *never* forgive her.

But my husband is here, and Dad won't tell this story in front of him. I appreciate that.

"Money makes a difference," I say. "I mean, Eileen doesn't have to work."

Two busboys appear, one carrying a circular tray nearly as large as the tabletop. The other snaps open a folding stand, and in complete silence they set down the tray and distribute our plates. We gape at the portion sizes. All three of us are the kind of people who can see the number of calories, and the numbers are comical.

The waitress asks if we'd like ketchup, mustard, Tabasco, red pepper, Worcestershire, barbecue, A-1, horseradish, and finally I interrupt her and say I think we're all set.

"Jesus," my father says when she's gone.

Jordan chuckles. He finds my father genuinely funny, though it's not completely clear whether he's laughing at him or with him.

"Give her a break," I say to Dad. "She's just doing her job."

"Actually, I do want ketchup for my fries," Dad says. He slips out of the booth, darts over to one of the busboy stations, and grabs a ketchup bottle off one of the low shelves.

"You two take some of these," he says when he gets back, and starts off-loading fries onto his bread plate.

"No way," I say. "Look at this." I point to my plate, which is the size of a hubcap and contains enough fettuccini Alfredo to feed all three of us.

"Jordan, I'm begging you," Dad says.

"I'll take some," my husband says. He's never been anything but nice to both my parents, and this means a lot to me. Most of the time I feel completely comfortable with my husband, but when we're around my parents I get paranoid about what he thinks of them. We've been married only a year, and there's still a lot we don't understand about each other.

My father accidentally drops a fry on the table, picks it up, and adds it to the heap he's offering Jordan.

"So what were we saying?" he says. "You think Eileen's lazy?"

"No!" I put down my fork. "God, where'd you get that?"

He grins gleefully. "You think Eileen's just sitting around all day watching soaps," he says, and Jordan chuckles again.

"That's not what I think," I say. "Maybe that's what you think."

"No, what I think," Dad says, "is that what's more important, even than money, is having two parents who love each other and get along and can laugh about stuff. What do you think, Jordan?"

"Sounds good to me," my husband says, but he's humoring him and that's probably obvious even to my father. Knowing he's being humored embarrasses him, and he'd probably be willing to drop the subject now, but I'm getting annoyed and stupidly want to keep it going.

"People don't get along when there's not enough money," I say to Dad. "If we're taking lessons from your life."

"Taking lessons from my life?" Dad asks. "I'm certainly not telling you to do that. I'm sorry, I just thought you two were all about living on love and poetry and rice and beans."

"That's what I'm about," Jordan says. He turns to me. "Don't you like rice and beans?"

"No," I say. "I'm going to need at least seventeen pounds of fettuccini Alfredo a day."

Dad picks up his heart-healthy turkey club. He looks at us for a second before he takes a bite, and smiles more to himself than to us.

"Life is funny," he says. Then he takes a huge bite of the sandwich and looks out into the restaurant as he chews.

What he means by this probably isn't fully clear even to him. But part of it has to do with some stereotype about men and women, about patterns, how things stay the same. Here we are, the newlywed Katie and Jordan, at thirty much older than he and my mother were when they got married, with all kinds of wisdom they didn't have. We're the redemption, the ones who won't make their mistakes. And yet, here's the young man not quite ready to settle down. The young woman screaming for money. Here's Katie turned into her mother after all.

"Life is funny to me too," I say.

Dad chews some more, then looks at us again. Before he speaks, he clears his front teeth of food, tongue bulging under closed lips. He takes a quick sip of wine.

"So did I tell you I'm going to the Super Bowl?"

"Nice," Jordan says.

"That's why I'm kind of trying to eat light, I mean if you can call this light. Hey, speaking of which." He looks at me. "Eat. You've hardly touched your food."

"Cause we're talking so much," I say.

And I'm suddenly angry, and also embarrassed of it. This change of subject is necessary, smart, civil, but also completely offensive. My father wants to bring up whatever he wants, whenever he wants, but then quit talking about it as soon as he doesn't like how the discussion goes. And Jordan's just going along with it, has no idea I'm angry, and if later I try to tell him, he'll get confused and defensive. It will make no sense to him that I'd be angry, because to him, this is just what parents do. They want grandkids. They think it'll be cute to see us all love-sick and sleep-deprived. When Jordan's parents do this, I know it doesn't occur to him to say to them, "I'll probably be a horrible parent, all right?" Or feel ridiculous with shame for thinking it.

"Anyway, it's pretty cool," Dad says. "I'll get to look back and say I saw Peyton Manning in the Super Bowl."

"That's awesome," my husband says.

"The company goes every year. From what I've heard, people get pretty wild."

"What does that mean?" I ask.

Dad and Jordan laugh a little. I didn't mean the question as a joke, but I'm glad that's how they're taking it.

"Wild for an old man," Dad says. "Oh, so speaking of old men." He looks at me. "I emailed your uncle Jimmy."

He pauses, giving me a little half smile, like I might know something about this. I don't.

"So doesn't he always have tickets for all the Indy teams?" Dad asks. "Don't you guys go to a Pacers game every time you're down there?"

"I mean, I don't," I say.

"He took us to the Pacers last year," Jordan says. "Yeah, he had courtside seats. Larry Bird was at the game. It was crazy."

"That's what I thought," Dad says.

He stares at Jordan for a second and flinches slightly, then nods. The nodding counterbalances some dark feeling, which he knows shouldn't be directed at Jordan but is.

The last time Jordan and I were in Indianapolis was for a wedding on my mom's side. Uncle Jimmy's daughter, actually. The morning after the wedding, we went over to my grandparents' for breakfast, and in the wide, empty streets of their retirement community, my brothers and uncles and male cousins played a game of tag football. Jordan played too. I sat on the lawn with my aunts, watching, and though I knew it was sappy I got a little teary seeing my husband out there with them. It was stupid, just a bunch of middle-aged guys horsing around with their teenage kids, their wives calling out things like, "Goddamn it, I am not driving you to the hospital if you sprain something." It could've been a prescription drug ad. But it made me happy.

If there was one person who could understand this kind of sentimentality, it was my father. But I didn't tell him. It would've hurt his feelings.

"So we were looking for a few more tickets," Dad says. "And I thought, what the hell. It's not like I wanted him to give them to me for free."

"What'd he say?"

"He never wrote me back."

The server is here again. She clasps her hands in front of her abdomen and asks how everything's tasting. Too loudly, my father says, "Great, thanks."

"What?" he says when she's gone. "Am I being rude?"

"I didn't say it."

"Hon," he says, "when you get to be my age, you realize you can only worry about so many people. If I went around all day worrying I'd offended every waiter and concierge and rental car guy, I would absolutely lose my mind."

"We wouldn't want that," I say.

"Which is why I don't care if I offended your uncle. I figured I'd seen him at your wedding, and things there were pretty friendly, and I might as well give it a shot. You think it was rude?"

"No."

"But?"

I have a third-hand story about my father running into Uncle Jimmy at a funeral years ago. An Indianapolis funeral, for the father of a guy they went to high school with. The man who'd died had lived in Dad's old neighborhood, just down the street. He'd once intervened when Dad's father came home blacked-out drunk and violent. My grandfather—Dad said you could see it on him a block away. You could hear it, even, in the sound of the front door's deadbolt, the key's teeth scraping in and out of the lock. Once, just after my grandfather threw open the door, this neighbor man appeared behind him on the steps. He was bigger than my grandfather and had three or four big sons just a few houses down.

"Jack," he called, "I wondered if you'd give me a hand over here. It's my car."

The neighbor glanced at Dad and his sisters, four skinny kids on the floor in front of the TV. Even then Dad knew there was nothing wrong with the neighbor's car. This man didn't save them forever from their mean, drunk father. But he did that day, Dad said, choking up when he told the story.

So at this man's funeral thirty years later, my father runs into Uncle Jimmy.

The way Jimmy tells it, he goes up to my father, says hello, and right away my father starts talking about how my mother is just bleeding him of money. How he can't sleep at night thinking about what's happened to his savings, his pension. You know what kind of car she drives now? he asked my uncle. And I pay her—and he told Uncle Jimmy the number. At the funeral. It was pathetic, my uncle said. It was embarrassing.

"Uncle Jimmy's really bitter," I say now.

"Is he?" Dad asks.

"Yeah, about Aunt Rita. About women in general. Last time we were down there, Mom asked if he was dating anyone. Guess what he said."

"Never again?"

"He said, 'They're all sluts.'"

"Jesus." Dad laughs a little. He turns his wineglass in his hands.

"So I don't think he's in a very generous phase."

"Or who knows?" Dad says. "Maybe he didn't even get my email."

Twenty years ago, when my mother married the man she'd left my father for, Uncle Jimmy refused to go to the wedding. This was probably more because he hated my stepfather than because he loved my father, but Dad took it as an act of loyalty. For years afterward, whenever he talked about my mother he'd include that detail. Even her own brother wouldn't go to that wedding.

"Are we thinking about dessert?" the waitress asks.

"I don't know," I say, but I give her a big smile and big eye contact, trying to communicate how friendly and well adjusted I am.

"Not me," Dad says. But then when Jordan and I decline, he insists we share at least one piece of cheesecake.

The cheesecake arrives, a smooth, white brick. The strawberry on top is the size of a small apple.

"I'm not having any," Dad says. "You two enjoy."

His hands are clenched into fists on the table again.

"Seriously?" I say. "We ordered it because you wanted it."

He shakes his head.

"You two can eat that and nothing will happen," he says. "I take a bite and I guarantee you—I guarantee you—I'll be five pounds heavier tomorrow morning."

"One bite?" I say.

"I'm telling you."

"You're crazy."

Jordan laughs. He waits for someone else to start eating first.

"Aging," Dad says. "You never really went to a funeral as a kid, did you?"

"A few in high school," I say. "Luke Fitzpatrick. Jonas Marzac."

"Right, those. God, that's awful. You only went to funerals for young kids. But we never took you to an open-casket wake for like a seventy-year-old guy, right?"

"Molly Toomey's dad," I say. "But it wasn't open-casket."

"And he was only in his forties."

Dad picks up a fork and scrapes off the thinnest ribbon of cheesecake.

"When I was a kid, I was always going to these wakes," he says. "Great-aunts and uncles, grandparents. Jesus, it seemed like once a month. And you had to go and kneel in front of the body. You know what I mean?"

I nod.

"Sometimes I look at my hands now," he says. "And I think, oh my God, my hands look like those corpses'. The skin's all spotty and loose. I can't describe it."

He holds up his free hand, which doesn't look corpse-like to me.

"It's just like, Christ," he says. "I'm closer to that than I am to childhood. A lot closer."

With my fork, I nudge the strawberry off the top of the cake and watch it plop onto the white plate. "Carpe diem, I guess," I say. "Right?"

"I'm not saying I'm going to die soon," he says. "Though who knows."

"I probably went to Grandpa Jack's funeral," I say. "Didn't I?"

Dad rests his fork on the edge of the plate.

"They cremated him," he says. "There was a memorial service in Indianapolis. I went but I didn't bring you."

"Did Grandma go?"

Dad shakes his head emphatically. "My sisters did," he says. "And me. The priest kicked it off, it was funny. Everyone's all quiet and somber, and the priest says, 'Now, I knew Jack pretty well, and I can tell you, he's going to be doing some time in purgatory.'"

He glances at Jordan and adds, "You know a little about my dad, don't you?"

"The Bozart Tavern?" Jordan says.

"Exactly," Dad says, and he smiles. It's an expression that often shows up in photographs of him and makes people ask, why didn't you smile? To which he says, that is a smile. I'm smiling.

If you met him now—or in the last couple years, like Jordan—you'd see him only as he is tonight. Completely bald, with glasses for farsightedness, beard flecked with white. You wouldn't know the beard was a fairly recent thing. You wouldn't, in the dim light of the Cheesecake Factory, be able to see the little childhood scar on his nose. You'd see: sport coat, no tie, phone clipped to belt—a businessman on the road. In decent shape for his age, but it's true, not like when he was young. This body, this collection of cells, is not what it used to be.

It was an angry young man my mother married thirty-three years ago. Angry at his parents' failure, the injustice of that and the world's indifference to it. He wanted to do better with his own kids. I used to be terrified of witches, and tucking me in at night, he used to say, "If any witch tries to come in here, you call me and I'll throw her out the window. I'll say, 'Get out of here, witch!'" Laughing, I echoed, "Get out of here, witch!" But when he left my room, he reentered the gigantic mortgage that was the rest of his life. His wife had stopped loving him, maybe after he stopped loving her. He didn't know whose fault that was.

This is a rough sketch of the truth. This is the best I can do.

"Tommy McLaughlin came to the service," Dad says. "That's always meant a lot to me, that he came. I went to his father's funeral, too. Did I ever tell you that?"

"I think so," I say.

"Just the check, please," Dad says to the server. And he says it warmly, politely, as if he's forgotten his aversion. Maybe he does this for me.

The last thing he tells us about is the birthday party he and Eileen threw for Simon a few weeks ago. Nine little boys in their kitchen, a small Lego set for each. Eileen had just finished telling them there was no eating in the living room when a redheaded boy picked up a handful of goldfish crackers and flung them into the living room. And thus began two hours of mayhem, stressful enough that the birthday boy at one point took his mother aside and asked if everyone could please go home. But a minute later he changed his mind and wanted them all to spend the night. It was funny to watch, Dad says, some kids had whole Lego battleships built in twenty or thirty minutes, while others could hardly snap two together without Dad's help. Some of them chewed on their Legos, which made Dad's teeth hurt just to think about. At some point Eileen caught two boys up in Simon's room, trying to break into his toy safe.

An hour into the party, Eileen and Dad considered opening a bottle of wine and refrained only because they were afraid what the other parents would think. And when the other parents finally came, the redheaded boy refused to go home. He hid behind the couch and hung onto the edge of the rug, and to get him out his father pretended there was a present for him in the car.

"Never again," Dad says. "Next year it's Chuck E. Cheese. I don't care if they charge me a thousand dollars."

Jordan and I laugh all through this story. I laugh harder than I have in a long time.

"I'm sure this really makes you want to have kids," Dad says.

"Oh, God," I say. "That's not what I'm afraid of."

The check comes, and I make a phony show of taking out my credit card. Dad flinches and tells me to forget it.

Out in the vast mall parking lot, most of the cars are gone. The edges of the lot are heaped with dirty snow. Probably because of the wine I've had, it doesn't feel as cold as it did before. For a minute, Dad can't remember what his rental car looks like, and he aims his key fob at a few different silver sedans before he finds it. We walk him over, stand in front of Macy's still-lit display windows, and say good-bye.

I watch as he and Jordan shake hands. For a strange moment, I feel like I don't really know either of them. But in some distant, maybe sentimental way, it makes me happy to see them together.

When they step apart, my father opens his arms to give me a hug.

"It was good to see you," I say, dropping my head onto his shoulder for just a second. "Call us next time you're in town."

"God," he says, looking at me with his wistful smile. "I feel like we hardly got to talk."

SHOPPING

I'd begun to feel profoundly sad whenever I spent time with my mother. Whenever she wasn't annoying me, that is, which was less and less now that I was in my thirties. I'd moved away and grown into the type of adult who goes to bed early, rises in the dark, and walks several miles alone, in all seasons, in streets empty except for a few delivery trucks. For most of my life, I'd been angry with my mother. I had thought that would change only if she changed. Now, without my intending it, the anger had disappeared, and in its place was this terrible sadness, an enormous, weather-like feeling, worse than the anger in that it seemed to have no acute cause.

Part of what made me sad was her back. She'd had scoliosis since childhood, but it hadn't been noticeable until recently, in her mid-fifties. She nursed a powerful bitterness toward her own mother for never taking her to have her back fixed. Or her teeth, though her teeth were more or less straight. One of her brothers had worn braces as an adult, and my mother had raged at me once, in the car on the way back from visiting my grandparents in Indiana, about how humiliated Jimmy must've been to have to walk the halls of his accounting firm with braces on his teeth. Any idiot knew there were a few things you did for your kids, to give them a prayer of becoming normal adults.

I defended my grandmother because I was in the habit of taking a contrary position with Mom, and because my grandmother had broken her hip that year and now had frequent pain and dragged her leg when she walked. Nana couldn't help it, I said. She and Pop-pop hadn't had much money.

You don't get it, my mother said. It wasn't the money. The woman was just completely oblivious. Mom thanked God I'd never know how it felt to be raised by someone so oblivious.

She was driving and I was riding in the passenger seat. Many of our conversations happen this way, so that when I try to picture my mother I often see her right profile rather than her whole face. She has exceptional bone structure, sharp clear shadows under each cheek. I look at her nose as she talks and observe that it really isn't large or unattractive, as she has thought all her life. When I was going through puberty, she told me that if I wanted she'd let me get a nose job. If I thought that would help with my confidence, she said. She has very sparse eyebrows, plucked when she was a teenager with a nervous compulsion she now regrets. As she drives, she uses the rearview mirror to isolate white hairs from her part, pulls them out, opens the sunroof, and releases them into the wind.

But her back. Its lopsided curve began to show a few years ago. It wasn't noticeable through her clothes, but I saw it sometimes in the dressing room at the department store where she spent a good part of her Sundays, looking for things to wear to court, to client dinners, to her law school reunion. She could've gone to a better law school, she knew now, but hadn't known it when, at twenty-four and pregnant with me, she sent in just the one application.

"I'm so stupid," she said today, addressing the words to the dressing-room mirror as I stood behind her trying to zip her into a dress. I was in town for the weekend; this was the last day of my visit.

"Don't say that," I said.

"Why?" she said. "I was stupid. I undersold myself."

"I don't like it when you call yourself stupid."

"Oh my God." She lifted her arms slightly, making an impatient face at me in the mirror. "You're misunderstanding. I don't mean I'm *stupid.*"

"OK, good," I said. I tugged the top corners of the zipper as close as they'd go.

"Stop," she said. "Don't tear it. I need to lose weight. I'm fat."

She pushed her fingertips into her belly, through the wool dress, and drew in a breath.

"Don't say that either," I said.

Through the dressing-room curtain, I knew that Sofie, the brisk, bone-thin saleswoman, who exercised a distinct ownership over my mother, could hear us and was probably annoyed, as I would've been in her place, by the psychological theater I'd brought to our shopping. But why should that bother me? Sofie's whole motivation was money. Emotionally dysregulated rich women were part of her job, as were, today, their scolding, sanctimonious daughters.

As if she'd heard me thinking, Sofie now spoke through the curtain.

"Maureen?" she said. "How we doing in there?"

My mother stepped away from me and opened the curtain. "She can't get it to zip."

Sofie didn't look at me. She reached out, large rings glitter-
ing on her long, elegant fingers, and touched the seams that ran
crookedly up the sides of my mother's waist.

"No," Sofie said, wrapping one arm around her own hollow
abdomen and raising the other hand to her face. She pursed her
mouth, took her hand from her face, plucked at the dress's left
shoulder. "No," she said again, this time with finality. "You need
a forty-two."

"I can't be a forty-two, Sofie," my mother said, half-joking but
also genuinely unhappy. "Please tell me I'm not a forty-two."

"This is Italian, Maureen," Sofie said. "Italian's different from
French. I'll show you the chart again."

"No, I know." My mother spoke like a chastised little girl.
"Bring the forty-two. Do you even have a forty-two?"

My mother wasn't fat. Her pale, hairless legs were still more
or less the ones the 1972 men's football coach at Cathedral High
School had pronounced the best of all the cheerleaders'. Hers,
the humble legs of a girl from Saint Agnes rather than one of the
more exclusive women's academies. Though she'd been accepted
to all of them. All of them. With a partial scholarship, even, at
Ladywood, but my grandmother had said it was still too expensive. What difference did it make? my grandmother had asked.
School is school.

"Don't stare," my mother cried when Sofie was gone. She'd
taken off the dress and now folded her arms over her bra.

"I'm not," I said, and then, against a resolution I try to keep,
added, "Jesus."

"I need to lose weight," she said. Keeping her arms crossed
coffin-style, she thrust back her shoulders, raised her chin, and
made a cold and critical face at herself. "Remind me to stand up
straight."

It was the scoliosis. There was nothing to be done about it. It was painful to see, even though it was subtle, because this aspect of her shame was so physical and could not by an adjustment of mind frame be banished.

And I had begun to believe, or at least hope, that the worst things could be banished in this way. I had quit drinking. After a very brief try with AA, I'd decided to do it on my own, using library books and a writing journal. I'd been sober two years, and had come to believe that any idea, even ones I'd once taken for laws, could be let go. Enemies and old lovers and sins let go like balloons by their strings. It was difficult, but also fantastically freeing. It was probably a vanity, but I wanted my mother to believe it too. But there, flouting me, was her unchangeable back.

"Maureen, look at me," Sofie said when she returned with the size forty-two dress. "You'll try this one. You don't like it, you don't buy it. Simple. But forty-two Italian is like American six. I'm sorry, eight."

"I know I'm not a six," my mother said. "I'm not delusional."

"Nobody's delusional," Sofie said. "You try this. I'll be back."

The dress fit, but my mother decided to have Sofie put it on hold. To this Sofie agreed with a tinge of hostility. I tried to give Sofie a sympathetic face but she still wouldn't look at me.

We crossed out of women's clothing and took the elevator up to the restaurant on the top floor. Facing my mother across the table, I couldn't see her scoliosis anymore. But the heavy, sad feeling deepened, as it often did immediately after she'd annoyed me.

"Will you make me a promise?" she asked.

"What is it?"

"Promise first. Will you promise?"

"Sure," I said. This was a familiar way for her to begin a conversation and I'd learned not to bother objecting.

"Will you not tell your brother what I said about Meg?"

"Of course I won't."

"You're going to tell," she said. "You have the biggest mouth."

An urgent little smile took over her face, and I knew she was trying to be conspiratorial, not accusing. But I'd outgrown my tolerance for this kind of intimacy. I looked down at my bread plate for a moment, then back at her with the most neutral face I could make.

"It hurts my feelings when you say that," I said.

"Oh, I'm kidding," she said. "Isn't that what the kids used to say about you? I'm kidding." She said the last sentence as if I'd lost consciousness and she was trying to revive me.

"OK." I looked at her steadily. "I'm glad to know you were kidding. I wasn't clear about it. Now I am."

"Oh my God," she said, rolling not just her eyes but her whole face toward the ceiling. "Why do you have to be like this?"

Our waiter, a pale, small man in his forties, approached our table.

"Will you tell my daughter she's being difficult?" my mother asked him.

He laughed timidly, glancing at me, then back at her. "I think I have just what you need," he said, and from the pocket of his white apron produced a leather-bound wine list.

"Exactly," my mother said, but he wasn't attractive enough for her to prolong the joke. Without looking at the list, she ordered her Kim Crawford. "Are you having one?" she asked me. "I never know what phase you're in."

"No, thank you," I said to the waiter, and thought of adding, *I've been sober two years.* But that would be retaliating. There was a difference between protecting oneself and retaliating, a subtle and important one I'd been late in learning.

"Very good," he said. "I'll put that in right away."

His computer station was only a few feet from our table, and as he stood there tapping the touch screen, his free hand resting on his cheek, I vacillated between shame and defiance. Surely we weren't the worst people he'd waited on. Like Sofie, this man held a job that by description included absorbing a fair amount of his customers' tedious dysfunction. Still, the hand on his cheek somehow filled me with remorse. It was the gesture of an anxious child. I imagined him nine years old—maybe he'd grown up like I did, with a houseful of kids and a rotating cast of exploited nannies, where televisions blared peacefully until the miserable, exhausted professional parents blazed in after bedtime and released their frustration in long, screaming, sometimes violent fights. I had stood once, perhaps with my hand on my cheek like that, with my ear to my closed bedroom door, my three younger siblings behind me on my twin bed, trying to hear what the police were saying to my stepfather, wondering whether they'd listen to him or my mother.

"You're staring," my mother said.

"He must hate working here," I said.

"I disagree. I'm sure this is a wonderful place to work."

"Will you do me a favor?" I asked.

"What?"

"Promise first."

"No," she said, but her face lightened as she understood my joke. "I'm not a sucker like you."

The favor I'd planned to ask was that she not, when the waiter returned, ask him how he felt about his job. But a better strategy was just to let the subject change.

"I would never tell Michael what you said about Meg," I said. "It'd just piss him off."

"I know you won't," she said. "I was kidding."

I had woken at five that morning and slipped out of my mother's house while she and her boyfriend and their little white terrier slept, and had walked twelve blocks to the lakefront. Now, as she resumed her verbose judgment of my brother and the moody, immature young mother of his three-year-old daughter, I remembered the colors that had sprawled over the sky just before sunrise. I'd stood on the bridge over Lake Shore Drive at North Avenue and watched the out-of-service buses lumber north to begin their routes, seeming to slip through the V of my legs in a kind of reverse birth. I'd felt the concrete bridge shudder in their wind.

". . . not in control of her temper at all," my mother was saying. "And I worry how it affects the baby. I do."

"That sounds hard," I said.

"That sounds hard?" Her thin eyebrows drew together, deepening the vertical crease between them, which she'd talked for months about having fixed. "When'd you start talking like this?"

"What do you mean?" I asked. "When did I start listening to you and responding to your feelings?"

The waiter appeared with her wine and set it silently in front of her. He seemed prepared to dissolve back into the restaurant, but my mother caught him first and ordered for us: two bowls of chicken soup and roasted vegetables to share.

"Healthy," she added. "We're watching our weight."

"Very good," he said.

"Well, she's not," she said. "She makes everyone in the dressing room feel bad. Come on, eat." She nudged the bread basket toward me, laughing, looking at the waiter. "I've got to fatten you up."

"I was saying," she said when he was gone, "it's not hard on *me*. It's not about me. I've noticed you take things so personally now. Like everything's about you."

I considered this, tried to show with my face that I was considering it. "That's probably true," I said. "I've been trying to pay attention to my feelings. A lot of alcoholics end up—"

"Don't call yourself that."

I didn't know if it had just started or if I hadn't noticed until now, but my heart rate had picked up suddenly, so much that it scared me a little. This is your sympathetic nervous system, I reminded myself. This is your body doing what it needs to do.

"Don't buy into these labels," she went on. "You don't have to go around saying, 'I'm an alcoholic.' "

I reached for my ice water, though my body felt suddenly cold and sipping the water made it colder.

"What now?" she said after a pause. "You're not speaking to me?"

The sun this morning had reflected off the north view of the city, the Hancock tower, the Drake Hotel. Taxis poured over the Drive like separate drops in a waterfall.

"Mom," I said.

"Are you shaking?" She looked incredulous now, furious, horrified, worried.

"I'm fine." I reached over the bread and touched her hand.

"Don't get your sleeve in that," she said. "It's oily."

"I'm cold," I said. "From the water. The water's making me cold."

"Here."

She slid out from her side of the table, the booth side, and pulled off her cardigan sweater. She came to my chair and draped the sweater around my shoulders. Then she took a step back and looked at me expectantly, as if waiting to see me transform. I felt the familiar embarrassment of being treated like a child in public, and because of where we were, the particular shame of being the cowed and spoiled daughter of a woman with money. For a moment I sat rigid, her sweater hanging insecurely from my shoulders. The childhood instinct was to fling it off, but instead I pulled the sweater closer around myself, fastened the top button over my collarbones. Then I smiled up at her. One of her hips was higher than the other.

"Is that better?" she asked.

"It is," I said. "Thank you."

"I'm going to tell them to turn up the heat."

She disappeared past my periphery. Though I faced the booth side of the table, where the faux leather was faintly darkened with the imprint of her back, I could in my head see her behind me, weaving through the tables, determinedly scanning for some inferior from whom she could demand redress of an imagined wrong. Telling them to turn up the heat was for her like having a drink used to be for me: quick, false relief of a large and frighteningly abstract pain. "Sir?" she'd be saying—I couldn't hear over the garble of crowd voices, the vague strains of Mozart from unseen speakers—"Sir?" with lawyerly assertiveness shallowly concealing a frantic need to be heard, deemed important, obeyed. "Sir?" Behind the booth were floor-to-ceiling windows, beyond which steel towers sentried the narrow, human-scale sidewalk.

"They said they'd turn it up," she said, sitting down in front of me again. The person she'd talked to must've flattered her with sympathy and attention, because she looked more than satisfied, looked genuinely happy. She was beautiful when she was happy. For all her fears, still a strikingly beautiful woman.

"It's ridiculous they'd have it that cold," she said.

"I love you, Mom," I said.

She refolded her napkin. Between our table and the bar, a decorative blue fire flickered soundlessly between twin panes of glass.

"What was that for?" she asked.

"I just wanted you to know."

"Of course I know," she said. "After lunch we can go look at jeans. Those ones you're wearing are ancient."

Our soup and vegetables arrived, ferried not by our waiter but by a tall, slender male subordinate. He nodded, murmured bon appétit, and was gone.

"He was cute," I said.

"Not my type," my mother said. "Isn't that strange? I know he's attractive, I can see that, but my—" She turned over her palm, held it out as if offering something. "Whatever you call it. It doesn't go off for that type."

"I know what you mean," I said.

"Chemistry," she said. "I get it from these arrogant types, the ones you can tell right away are going to treat you like shit. I mean, come on. Mike Durkin?"

My ex-stepfather. They'd divorced when I was fourteen.

"What was I thinking?" she said. "It was like I knew. Like I scanned for the nastiest, most sadistic man in the room, zeroed in on him, and said to myself, 'That's him. That's the one you want. Maybe before you're through he'll break one of your bones. Which bone do you think it'll be?'"

The waiter, the original one, came by to check on us. Everything was wonderful, my mother told him, and then asked him to thank the manager for turning up the heat.

"Your father wasn't that much better," she continued when he was gone. "I know you don't like hearing that, but it was all the same pattern. These arrogant, angry—you could see it in his face all the time. I mean even when he was happy. Just this anger. I'm sorry."

I shook my head.

"I'm *sorry*," she said again. "You're giving me that face."

"I'm just listening."

"I shouldn't be talking about this with you."

She picked up her soupspoon and started to eat, leaning in to blow on each spoonful, using her free hand to hold back her hair. Between bites she looked off to one side, eyes moving only to blink. I knew she was seeing some scene from the past, some terrible moment I'd witnessed, which she wanted me to affirm, or one I hadn't witnessed, which she wanted me to understand. Once, at eleven years old, I'd gone downstairs and gotten between my stepfather and her, had screamed at him in my child's pitch, *leave her alone, leave her alone.* Once, at twelve, babysitting and nursing a can of Coke laced with bourbon from their sideboard, I'd spilled scalding hot soup on my little half brother's legs and given him second-degree burns. Now it was twenty years later. We were sitting in the top-floor restaurant of a fancy department store.

"It's because of my dad," she said, turning back to me suddenly. "He was in a bad mood all the time, too. Probably because my mother was such a pain in the ass."

She took another bite of soup and sniffed out a laugh.

"I'm kidding," she said. "I know you don't like it when I talk about her."

"They're your feelings," I said, but as the words came out I was flooded with awareness of my incompetence. I knew a few cheap principles from commercial self-help, and with those thought I could heal—what? What did I think?

"It's stupid," she said. "She's a crippled old woman. You can't spend your life on this stuff."

"It's not stupid." The sadness was spreading up my neck to my jaw. It tinged the air in the restaurant like a faint humidity. I didn't want a drink but was conscious that a drink would erase this feeling, and I had to believe that if that were the case, other things could erase the feeling also. The sun rising over Lake Michigan. The waves. The separate joggers on the paved path, private in their exertion, stoic or scowling, alone. My mother was right. You couldn't spend your life on this stuff. Everyone was in pain, most of it much worse than mine.

My mother plunged her fork into a halved Brussels sprout, furrowed as a brain, glistening with oil.

"Do you think I should get that dress?" she asked.

"It looked really good on you," I said. "You looked really pretty."

"Oh, stop," she said, and looked at her plate. She shook her head. "It's too expensive."

"Can I ask you something?" she asked later, when we were in the car again, driving to Union Station to drop me at my train. She'd taken Michigan Avenue, and though I was relieved to be leaving, I regretted seeing the landmarks pass, the old water tower, the InterContinental Hotel, where a throng of blue satin bridesmaids was being consumed by the slow revolving door. Cityfront Plaza, where my father used to have a cubicle, though he hardly used it because he traveled so much, and the Tribune Tower, and the big, cold river engineered to flow backward, in from, not out to, the lake. I was looking east, through my mother's side of the windshield. Her blurred profile kept pace with everything I saw.

"Sure," I said. We'd caught the stoplight at Lake Street.

"Do you think your brother is like that?" she asked. "Like them, I mean. Angry."

"I don't," I said. "I really don't."

"I worry about it."

I looked farther ahead now, still east, toward the new structures of Millennium Park, none of which had been there when I lived in the city. For some reason, I couldn't picture what had been there before.

"He was such a sweet kid," I said. "Remember how sweet he used to be?"

"But now is he?"

There had been a construction site in the park for a long time. This was crazy, that I couldn't think back farther than that.

"I think he is, Mom," I said.

I was crying. I had thought I could wait until I was on the train, slipping quietly out of the tunnel, in public-private with my face to the window. The stoplight changed, we started moving again, and the gaudy silver spectacle of the new park rolled out beside us.

"What's wrong?" my mother asked.

She was crying also. For a minute we both cried, and laughed because we were crying, and then cried a little more.

"Jesus Christ," she said, wiping her face. "We better stop or I'll wreck the car."

We turned right and passed under the El tracks, into the Loop, in silence. It was dimmer now under the shadows of the buildings. We crossed the river again, this time at the south branch.

"You can drop me here," I said, but she wouldn't stop until we'd gone all the way around the block to the station's main entrance.

"It's such a beautiful building," she said.

"It is."

"Do you miss it? Living here?"

"I do," I said, because she wasn't looking for a longer answer.

"When will you be back?"

"I'll have to see. Christmas for sure."

"Come sooner. I'll buy your ticket. I don't mind."

HERE FOR

Last night I dreamed I was screaming for my mother. The dream came after my son had called out to me, I have no idea what time. My only clock is my phone and I try not to look at it at night. I went and lay down with my son, fell asleep in his bed for a few minutes or hours, then woke and went back to mine.

Then I dreamed I was screaming for my mother, with a kind of need I can't feel in waking life, so pure and totalizing it has a color but the color has no name. I don't know.

Sometimes the screams were barely audible, and in the dream I was desperately gathering strength to make them loud. Sometimes it worked.

Then my alarm, which is my phone, went off. In bed next to me, my husband either slept through the alarm or pretended to. I shut it off, rolled onto my stomach, and masturbated. My husband either slept through it or pretended to. I was quiet, and it was quick. Then I got up.

My friend Jeffrey's dad died about a month ago. We talked for the first time last weekend, just texting, while I sat in my car in the driveway waiting for my son to wake from his nap. My son is three years old. As he sleeps in his car seat, his lower lip puffs out, petal red and wet with drool.

Jeffrey was there when his father died. He flew on a red-eye to make it in time, and he did make it, by just a few hours. They were long hours, Jeffrey says. Sitting around the hospital, thinking it could happen any minute or not happen at all. Then, afterward, it was like no time had passed.

Like giving birth, I text him, and then quietly panic that I've said something awful.

He writes, *Exactly.*

I get tears in my eyes.

It's the perfect *exactly*, I think, waiting for him to write again. Exactly as inexact as what I just said. He doesn't know what I'm talking about and I don't know what he's talking about, but there's a mutual will to believe each other.

Or maybe it's just a pass, him knowing I don't know the right thing to say. No one does, and he's too tired to give tutorials on grief support.

It's good that you— I begin, but then his next text comes in and I delete mine.

It sounds like a bad movie scene, he says. Maybe even a good movie scene, but he swears when his dad died it was like years of anger and disappointment dissolved. He was crying. All year he'd been crying about his dad, in counseling with Gaby, who went with him so he didn't have to go alone. But this crying was different, it was so—

Unembarrassed, I think, because the word is right in front of me, in his text message. Still, I encounter it as if I had thought it first.

I could just let go, Jeff writes. *I know that sounds—*

He writes more, a lot more, and I'm glad he's telling me, I want him to. I want to interrupt and tell him I love him, that my husband loves him, that we're here for him, whatever *here for* means. I don't interrupt; my excess of love is off topic. I listen—text-listening, which means I can turn around to check on my son, who is utterly still. A drawing teacher once told me portraits of children don't count as portraits. Children are too featureless, too much like apples. This was high school, the teacher a priest.

Unembarrassed, I think later, at the sink washing dinner dishes. My son's in the living room shooting my husband with a cardboard tube, singing the weapon's sound: "P'chew, p'chew!"

My mother has fatty tumors in her arms. The last time we visited her in Chicago, she made me feel them.

"See?" she said. She pushed up her sweater sleeve and extended her freckled forearm. I gently squeezed, first near her wrist, then up by her elbow, and felt the little lumps around the bone. "But they don't change at all," she said. "I think that's good, that they don't change at all."

"Definitely," I said.

She's a lawyer, has an office in a skyscraper. Pilots her black BMW down the Kennedy Expressway every morning, blows the on-ramp stoplight because she doesn't believe in it. I used to know a lot of people with parents like this.

A woman my mother knows socially is sexually open in a way that stresses her out. "Every time I see her, she hugs me," my mother said on that last visit, the same day she showed me her tumors. "But then she, like, rubs her breasts against mine, I swear. It's like this," she said, and grabbed me, and showed me.

"Mom," I said.

"I'm sorry!" she cried. "But that's what it's like, it's so uncomfortable!"

My mother is sixty-two. Once, in a box of her old things, I found her teenage diary. Entry after entry, in plump, pretty cursive, were earnest prayers that she would make the cheerleading team. Then an entry announcing she'd made it, with promises to God to be good and do all he asked of her. After that, the book is blank.

A few women I know get tipsy and inhabit a character with brittle, loud laughter telling awful stories. They swallow a drink and say in front of everyone at the party, "It'd be different if my mother had loved me," then laugh and dig their nails into my arm.

It's acting. I like it.

I say, "I know, baby. I know."

I know a little about their parents. Bonnie's mother laid her down on the counter when she was nine and tried to cut her hair with a kitchen knife. Bridget's mother showed Bridget *The Exorcist* to make her go to church. There are so many personality disorders to read about. Each of us is hurting the most. Each of us is fine.

AMENDS

Lizzie had known she would eventually get a call from Andy
Molloy. It was the first thing she'd thought when she heard
he was in AA. But by the time the call finally came she'd mostly
stopped thinking about it, and so felt surprised and even tender
when she heard the message he left, with its flat Chicago vowels and awkward, somber tone. He didn't need to apologize, she
thought. But it was sweet.

When she heard the message, she was standing in the parking
lot behind her apartment building in Seattle. Cell phone recep-
tion was bad in the apartment, so she'd gone outside to check her
voicemail, waiting first to finish dinner with her husband. From
the parking lot, concrete stairs led down to a narrow through
street, railed off along its west edge, and past that was a steep
drop to I-5. Beyond, the setting sun bleached a hole in orange
clouds above Queen Anne.

She called back immediately and, as she listened to the phone
ring, walked down the concrete stairs, running her hand along
the corroded pipe railing. Halfway down, the stairs forked

around a grassy hill. On the south side of the stairs two men sat drinking from bottles in paper bags, so she went north.

A generic female voice answered her call: she'd reached the voicemail of—and then, in his own voice, his name pronounced carefully and slowly. Andy Molloy, more a concept than a person. Lizzie was proud of how calm she felt, how gentle.

Across the grass she could see the men, young men, their hands and arms covered in tattoos. She thought of them listening as she began her message. And maybe they were, though they were talking, not loudly but with an easy, cursing fluency that made her want in the faintest way to join them. She was speaking warmly to Andy Molloy's voicemail. It was so nice of him to call, she said, and please—there was no need to apologize.

She could feel the facial expressions she was making more than she could feel her hand moving down the metal rail or her feet picking over the crumbled, root-split stairs. She felt her eyebrows lift in emphatic sincerity and the sad, generous smile that gave shape and melody to her speech. Really, she said, really, really, really. When she made her way to a natural close—the message long enough, but not too long—and when she held the phone away from her head and tapped the red end-call button, she was still smiling, moved by the ritual, an old one, of penitence and absolution. And she was also a little embarrassed.

Because, though none of this was ungenuine, it wasn't exactly honest either. She had known since she'd heard Andy Molloy was in AA that she'd eventually get this call, and had known also that she would forgive him. And her forgiveness was not ungenuine, not inside the dome of ideas in which she'd lived most of her life. She checked the screen of her phone to make sure she'd ended the call properly, and then, just to be safe, shut the phone off completely.

It wasn't that she was angry with Andy Molloy. She'd never been angry, only embarrassed. The particular circumstances of the incident had made it a little more like rape than some people would be comfortable with, but then again, come on. Drunks blacked out and had bad, regrettable sex. She and Andy Molloy both knew that. These men on the stairs—above her now, as she crossed the empty little street above the highway—knew it too. She felt like asking them. Like friends, they'd say it back to her, what she already knew was true.

She wished she could have a real conversation with Andy Molloy about what they had in common. They'd been kids together, never really friends but part of the same erratic adolescent social frenzy. She remembered sitting stoned in the bleachers of the school gym as hundreds of feet pounded, rattling the planks under her, a wild, nonsensical noise growing faster and faster, and under it the wheezing joints of the bleachers' metal supports. It rose to a dome under the high gym ceiling till it burst and rained down on their hundreds of heads like invisible confetti. A massive crucifix hung high on the south wall.

She wanted to know if Andy Molloy remembered all that, how he felt about it now. If it had scared him a little, the way it had scared her. But that wasn't what he'd called to talk about.

The sun seemed to become even brighter as it dropped. It was late summer but the weather here was never really hot, and the metal rail above the highway was cold where she rested her wrists. The concrete steps would be cold on the men's legs also, even through their jeans, if they weren't too drunk to feel it.

"Cause fuckin' that'd be too fuckin' *easy*," one of them said.

"Right?" the other answered.

Andy Molloy had once taken her by the shoulders, from behind, in the quiet of a full classroom, as the clock snipped away the seconds of a science quiz. She had been paralyzed. Her smooth-running mind was stopped. Male hands on her shoulders in the neutral public of a working classroom. Like something from a sex dream, the sudden damp desire, discolored by humiliation. He was pushing her slowly to one side of her chair. Trying to cheat off her paper, she realized after a delay. When she understood, she moved for him.

They had been fourteen. None of it had been personal. She felt this now, as she gazed at I-5, listening to variations in its gray stream of noise, listening to the drunk men. Male hands on her shoulders from behind. Like predator's venom, it stiffened her, softened her. Paralysis not quite unwelcome. When she was fourteen, she'd used this over and over, alone in her little twin bed at her mother's.

Ad majorem Dei gloriam, stenciled in gold paint above the classroom door, under the tsking clock. None more susceptible than a lapsed Catholic to the rhetoric of twelve-step. *We admitted we were powerless.* She'd tried it herself. The summer after Pat Degnan's wedding, when she still lived in Chicago. Plastic chairs and awful stories. Woman after woman, all versions of the same. Most of them worse. She'd wept heavily for them, but sat stiffly, not liking her spine to sink into the plastic chair's molded curve. Stiff and gripping a wad of tissues silky with lotion. Suffering was commonplace. And those greasy tissues absorbed almost nothing.

Now she held her phone tightly, not wanting to drop it over the ledge. The power was off. He could not call her back.

Her husband, up in the apartment, Mahler on the record player, wouldn't want to hear about Andy Molloy. For honesty's sake she'd tell him, but she didn't want to. He loved her and would try to understand but wouldn't like it.

In the little twin bed at her mother's she used to lie facedown, face crushed into the pillow hot with breath. Green lights inside her crushed eyelids. The dog scrambled under the bed when her mother and stepfather started fighting downstairs. The dog always heard it just before she did, the first dry thunder of their anger. Then screaming, things breaking. Very rarely police, who did at least help calm things down.

But she was thirty-one years old now and knew how commonplace it was. Boozy theater in downstairs rooms, the brute second husband, close shot of a woman's fingers on phone keys, *he pushed me.* Lizzie almost missed feeling alone in it. The dull, private rage those bland high school mornings, being flip to the homeroom teacher, cold to her friends. It had made her unusual to herself, less of a child.

The men on the stairs quit talking when she turned around and started back. She watched them as she climbed the north side of the steps, two skinny marionettes in black. The man nearest to her lifted his elbow and cocked his neck to drink. Then he lowered the paper-covered bottle from his mouth and, seeing her looking, lifted it toward her with a nasty smile.

She smiled back. Not mildly. She could look at whomever she wanted.

He looked surprised, then grinned. One tooth was a little gray. He extended the bottle farther toward her.

"Hey," he called as she continued up the steps.

Her pulse knocked in her ears, but she didn't hurry.

"Hey, you," the other started in.

She was past them now, couldn't see them without turning. Heat spread up her chest, her neck and head, and she was damp under her arms. But she could move, foot by foot, up the mossy concrete. They were howling after her, and at this she laughed, and turned her head to show them she was laughing, but her eyes were half-shut, the men blurred. The one she'd smiled at swished the air with his hand as if trying to pull her back.

She'd almost reached the parking lot. It was noticeably colder up here. The descending sun burned in the back windows of her apartment building, but no heat seemed to reach them. What had she said in her message to Andy—she hardly remembered, though it'd been less than five minutes ago. She didn't remember the words, only the tenderness she'd put on like a costume. He shouldn't feel—he didn't need to— But it hadn't felt like a costume. She did forgive him, if there was such a thing.

No one could really believe in God now, but they all still believed in forgiveness. At seventeen they had gone in groups, in a yellow school bus, away to be forgiven. In the parking lot of a retreat center up near the Wisconsin border, in enforced silence, they had filed off the bus, dragging small suitcases over the paved walk into a low, homely brick building with all its plain, thick curtains drawn. Enforced silence in the halls. Spare, Christless crosses above the door to each narrow dormitory room, and folded army blankets on stiff white bedsheets. The silence was meant to seep slowly into their thoughts, drying pools of transience with the cold heat of the eternal. Mildly fearful, they were herded into a large, plain room to sit on metal chairs.

The first speaker was one of their English teachers. A pink-faced man with prematurely white hair, alumnus of the school, assistant to the women's basketball coach. Lizzie had him her freshman year; his big joke had been, "Shall I compare thee to a summer's day? Nah, I got better things to do."

They didn't know what sin was, he said now. They had no idea. Stealing, cheating, killing—that was easy. If they thought that was all sin was, they were lying to themselves, like adults lie to kids who can't understand the truth. Well, it was time to quit being kids. The face of sin was not some leering mug shot; it was in the mirror. In the lies they told themselves. The secret lusts and hatreds. Look around the room, he told them. Notice. The small, cruel judgments they made about each other. Their superiority, their cowardice. If someone they loved was being hurt, would they have the courage to stop it, to speak up? No. And if they thought yes, they were liars. They didn't look in the mirror, because if they did, they'd have to change. And that took courage. And they didn't have it.

And it was bullshit. She knew it then, in the moment—she'd been taught about rhetoric, indoctrination. But he expected resistance, he said. In fact, resistance was a sign, because those most in need of God's forgiveness were those who feared it most. But no—it was bullshit. She knew this trick too, and her heart started to pound as she fantasized standing up from her chair, walking out—*and that took courage*—but now the English teacher was finished. The lights in the room were lowered, and at the back of the room the door slowly opened again.

At first they could see only the long empty hall. Then out of the dark appeared a boy from Lizzie's chemistry class. A lanky, stooping boy with terrible acne, crusted and peeling with medication, but in the dark this was harder to see. He stood in the doorway, stiff as a priest, both hands holding a burning candle in a glass.

He proceeded down the aisle between the chairs, his chest thrust forward and his chin solemnly tucked. She could see that he was trying not to rush, though his body seemed to want to. He put his candle on an altar at the front of the room, then took his place at the podium, where his printed speech had already been placed.

AMENDS *177*

His name was Kevin. Some of them knew him, he said, and some had only seen him in the halls. Most of them probably didn't know that his mother had left his family when he was nine years old and had since then been in and out of mental hospitals. His father had done his best to raise two sons, but his older brother had ended up fighting a serious drug addiction. Kevin knew that most of them, his friends and classmates, though they saw him every day at school, could never have known this about him.

He paused to turn the page, and then raised his head and looked out shyly at the audience. Lizzie felt she'd never seen his face before. In the candlelight, his acne looked like the shadow of a beard and made him seem older than the rest of them. He had clear, earnest eyes, visible now with his hair combed back. In a trembling voice, he told them how he'd tried to commit suicide. In bad, halting metaphors, he described how the world had seemed, and his awkward, melodramatic words made him that much more tragic: he could not say it, but she understood.

Another of their teachers, a plainclothes nun, had come around, silently offering packets of tissues. He had thought—and here the boy paused again and stood utterly still. He didn't stammer or start to cry, but just stood there, shoulders back, chin tucked, eyes on the podium, for a few long, empty seconds. In candlelight he was the photographic negative of himself. When he spoke again, he didn't start the sentence over, but went on as though he hadn't stopped—*it might be easier.*

After that she'd gone along with all of it. She'd penciled her sins on slips of white paper and burned them with the others' in a fire in a brass urn. Wept till she felt bleached. Hugged people, teachers, classmates she'd never talked to.

But she wasn't seventeen now. Behind her apartment building, the angle of the sun changed and the bright, burning windows became dull again. It was too cold to stand out here without a jacket.

She crossed the rows of parked cars into the gangway at the side of her building. As she let herself in the side door she thought she heard one last shout from the men on the stairs. But no, she must have imagined it. They were too far away.

Maybe she could explain it to her husband by beginning with the boy named Kevin who at fifteen had bought a long nylon rope from which to hang himself. Everyone suffered. Most of them worse. She came from a place where you weren't permitted to forget it. And so some ended up maniac drunks. Some ended up sex addicts. She meant it when she told Andy Molloy he didn't have to ask her forgiveness.

Forgiveness for what? Pat Degnan's wedding?

She pulled the door shut behind her and stepped into the hall. At a normal pace she passed the unmarked doors to the laundry and bicycle storage, passed the bank of mailboxes, curved into the main lobby. She started up the stairs, following a path in the diamond-patterned carpet. Pat Degnan's wedding had been five years ago. They'd all still been kids. Her husband, who two flights up was reading peacefully on the sofa, had not existed yet.

Nonsense of youthful voices in a bad spring break bar. An all-I-got-was-this-lousy-T-shirt town, gulf side of Florida. The girls she'd rented a condo with had been angry with Andy Molloy, but she'd only been embarrassed. Beauty of the blackout, only pieces of it stuck. Pat Degnan's bride coked up and chewing up her lips, heeling like a sailboat on her barstool. Sun-scorched groomsmen, dress shirts off, neckties still on. Male hands on her shoulders.

Lizzie passed the shut doors of other apartments. Over the years she'd lost track of those girls. Even the one who'd come looking for her that night at Andy's hotel. She'd asked them not to tell her, but they had anyway. When her friend came to find her, she was naked in the shower, where Andy had tried to put her after she vomited. She was screaming, they said, crying, banging on the glass shower door. In the hall of her apartment, she shut her eyes and breathed out a little laugh. At least she hadn't broken the shower door, only bruised herself and not badly. He didn't have an STI or anything. Embarrassed, not angry. The girls had tried to make her feel—but how? She had too much in common with him.

She checked the number on her apartment door before she slid the key into the lock. Doors all alike and once in a while she mixed them up. The key wouldn't turn. Ah, she'd left it unlocked. Through the door she could hear that he'd changed the music to Bach.

What kind of ridiculous person would be bitter about such a standard adolescent thing? He'd said he hoped contacting her would not cause further harm. Language of the book, she'd read it too. All of it just out of some book.

She pushed the door in slowly. Bright, furious organ music burst from the apartment like logomanic speech. He hadn't heard her come in, and as she slipped out of her shoes she enjoyed a few last minutes of invisibility. What she'd say to her husband began to take form in the music-thick air. Religion dead. Past past, burned up behind you like a field. He wouldn't quite believe her—it was more complex than that. Fine, but hers was the lesser of two stupidities. She'd been dishonest with Andy Molloy because he wouldn't understand her honesty. He didn't have to be sorry. He didn't have to cry in front of strangers. His guilt did no one any good.

She put her phone and keys in the dish on the front hall table, came around the corner to the living room. Her husband sat far to one side of the sofa, reading, not looking up. She crossed the room to lower the volume on the record player. The windows on that wall faced east, into the street, the opposite direction from the parking lot.

"So this was strange," she began.

He held up a finger, eyes still on the book. He used his other hand to turn the page.

She faced the window again. They'd been married a year. Some days she felt so close to him it was like they were one person.

"Sorry," he said after a minute. "I just wanted to finish that section."

"Of course," she said. "Don't apologize."

ACKNOWLEDGMENTS

First, I can't thank Anne Strother enough for the many generous ways she's supported this book. Same to Laurie Cedilnik, Bridget Dooley, Rachel Kincaid, Elissa Cahn, and Elizabyth Hiscox, whose depth, sensitivity, and humor were invaluable during my years at Western Michigan University.

Enormous thanks also to my teachers there, Thisbe Nissen, Nancy Eimers, T. Geronimo Johnson, and Bill Olsen, for insight, honesty, and friendship. Also to my incredible teachers at University of Washington—Maya Sonenberg, Shawn Wong, Charles Johnson, David Bosworth, Richard Kenney, and David Shields. And above all to Daniel Orozco, whose encouragement and influence have meant the world to me.

Deepest thanks to Parneshia Jones for believing in this book and in me, and to everyone at Northwestern, especially Anne Gendler, Olivia Aguilar, and JD Wilson, who've been truly delightful to work with.

I'm profoundly grateful to my agent, Maria Massie, for generous guidance and support every step of the way.

Thank you so much, Margaret Noel, for the beautiful cover image.

So many brilliant, talented writers have supported my work through ongoing conversation, feedback, friendship and community: Lacey Jane Henson, Patrick Somerville, Katie Ogle, Maggie Vandermeer, Kara Norman, Olivia Clare Friedman, Mark Rader, Nancy Jooyoun Kim, Peter Mountford, Pattabi Seshadri, Gretchen Kalwinski, Hannah Pittard, Pete Coco, Jonathan Messinger, Scott Stealey, and Jennifer Gravley.

I've been indelibly affected by decades of love and friendship with Alexis Jaeger, Sarah Hilliker, Jennifer VanEekeren, Meghan Graber, and Patrick Hennessey.

Endless thanks to my family—Mom, Dad, John, Anne, Johnny, Ellen, James, Owen, Maura, Sam, Rocío, Ruby, Cary, Abbey, and all of the Kriegs—for so much love and support. I am so lucky.

And finally, to Brandon, my love, my heart's home, and Ezra, our sweet son. I could not have written this book without you.